LS92

Billy Morris

ISBN: 9798785856363

Print Edition

LS92 is a work of fiction. The characters, with the exception of named football personalities, are fictitious. Any similarity to real persons, living or dead, is entirely coincidental and not intended by the author. Where 'real-life' named individuals appear, the situations, opinions, history and dialogues relating to those persons are entirely fictional and are in no way intended to depict or reflect actual events or facts.

The author can be contacted at
BM.Author@outlook.com

Billy Morris was born in Leeds, Yorkshire in 1966. He left Leeds in the late 1990's and has lived and worked in Europe and USA. He now lives in the Philippines. He wrote his first book 'Bournemouth 90' in 2021.

Accents, Dialects and Pronunciation

LS92, and its predecessor Bournemouth 90, are set in Leeds, a city in West Yorkshire in the North of England. The Leeds accent could generally be described as 'Yorkshire' but is quite distinct, and is easily identifiable when compared to speech in other parts of the county. Even different areas of the city have their own distinct dialects.

People in Leeds have a tendency to miss out letters, join words together and speak quite quickly. It's not an exaggeration to say that a conversation between Leeds folk could sound like a foreign language when compared to 'BBC English.'

Including dialogue exactly as it would most likely be spoken would therefore make this book unreadable for many people. However, there are certain fundamental elements of the Leeds accent which I felt needed to be reflected, in order to maintain a level of authenticity in the characters' speech. The following substitutions have therefore been made throughout the book-

The most obvious is the dropping of the word 'the' before a noun. In Leeds 'the' will be replaced by what linguists call a glottal stop. Execution of this element of the Leeds accent is generally difficult for a non-Yorkshire native. Actors on TV and in films usually get it wrong by either missing out 'the' entirely, or pronouncing a 't' in its place. As a Leeds speaker, I can't even explain how to execute a glottal stop. Google tells me it's achieved by rapidly closing the vocal chords. I've no idea how you do that. If you want to hear an example, I suggest you listen to an interview with David Batty or Kalvin Phillips. They're both experts. In the book, a glottal stop to replace 'the' is denoted by an apostrophe (').

"We're going to the pub' would therefore become "We're off to' pub".

Owt, Nowt and Summat – The words anything, nothing and something will usually be replaced by owt, nowt and summat by a native Leeds speaker. Owt is usually pronounced 'oat', nowt is pronounced 'note', summat is 'summert'.

I recognise it may be confusing to include speech patterns which are unrecognisable beyond the boundaries of West Yorkshire, but I felt that dialect would become unrealistic in the context of the stories without at least including these substitutions. I hope this doesn't impact on your enjoyment of either of the books.

Chapter 1

Monday 13 April 1992

Inspector Andy Barton reached across the passenger seat of the unmarked Cavalier and rummaged in the glove box. He removed a folded copy of the Evening Post and passed it to the young man beside him, then continued in his search. The passenger shuffled sideways, raised his chin above the zipped-up collar of his Henri Lloyd jacket, and glanced at the back page headline.

Magnifique! - Eric Cantona, French darling of the Leeds United supporters, today basked in the glory of his wonder goal against Chelsea at Elland Road. 'Ooh-ah-Cantona' is the latest cult chant at Leeds. His extrovert skills are sending the fans wild, and their joy erupted after his superb goal in Saturdays 3-0 win.

"Fuck's that for?" The young man nodded towards the handheld cassette recorder that Barton had retrieved from the glove box.

"New rules. All informant interviews have to be taped to be admissible as evidence. PACE. Load of bollocks, but it has to be done I'm afraid."

"No names though right?" The young man wound down the car window and flicked his cigarette butt over the parapet of the Merrion Centre multi-storey.

Andy Barton simultaneously pressed the 'play' and 'record' buttons and winked.

"Monday, 13th of April 1992, 8.43am, Acting Inspector Barton interview with criminal informant 'Hunter'."

"Hunter?" The young man shook his head and smirked.

"I had to think of something. It could be like, you know, hooligan hunter or something."

"For fuck's sake. Let's just get on with it. What do you want?" The young man tugged his zip up to its highest point and burrowed his chin deep in his coat.

"I need something." Andy Barton drummed his fingers on the steering wheel and stared ahead, as a Capri slalomed up the ramp towards the level above, tyres screeching on the concrete.

"Summat like what? I can't just magic stuff up if nowt's happening."

"That's not the right answer." Andy Barton continued staring ahead, the hum of the tape recorder the only sound to break the awkward silence.

"I've nowt to tell you though..." The young man mumbled into his coat, hands buried deep in the pockets as he slumped defensively in the passenger seat.

"You know the deal," Andy Barton turned to face him, voice now raised. "You'd have gone down. You know that. You were offered a way out and you took it. There's no backing out now. You've given me nowt for months."

"Because there's fucking nowt happening." The young man puffed out his cheeks and nodded at the tape recorder. Andy Barton pushed the stop button.

"You understand how it works," Barton sighed and looked out of the side window at the oil stained grey concrete. "If the bosses invest, they want to see results. Something to talk to' press about. It's been great since Bournemouth, football intelligence is the new buzz phrase. Money's been no object, but they want some payback now, and I'm under a lot of pressure."

"Bournemouth was a one-off. A mad weekend on' piss. Most of' lads down there hadn't been to a game for years. There is no organised hooligan firm, never was. Those days are over. You lot have spoilt it for yourselves-made yourselves redundant. Cameras everywhere, banning orders. No one wants to get done now. Especially when we might actually win summat this season." The young man lit another cigarette and exhaled smoke through the open window.

"I need something. My gaffer needs to justify the amount they've put into the team. He wants another Wild Boar."

"Fucking hell. I bet you've even had meetings to think up a new name..."

"Man U in' league cup at' Wheatsheaf. That wasn't an accident. Their FIO says someone over here arranged that. Spurs away last month. Whose idea was it to walk down from Seven Sisters at 3.15 when the pub got smashed up? Someone's still calling the shots..."

"Are they fuck!" The young man burst out laughing, sending a cloud of smoke billowing into Andy Barton's scowling face. "You're living in' past. There's no Mr.Big, no hooligan general. If it kicks off now, it's mostly likely an accident. Two mobs of lads meeting by chance."

"You fucking listen to me. I'm turning this tape back on and I want some names. If I don't get them, I'll personally make sure you go down for your original charges, and some. Understand?"

Andy Barton pressed 'Play' and 'Record' and the silence was again broken by the mechanical hum of the cassette recorder.

The young man nodded slowly and blew smoke rings through the window into the damp gloom of the multi-storey.

"So 'Mr.Hunter' are you able to provide the names of individuals who have been involved in recent incidents of football related disorder?"

The young man paused, then spoke slowly.

"Carl Elliott, Jamie Clifford, Rob Slater."

Andy Barton nodded.

"That's good, useful. Three's not going to be worth a full squad getting up at 4am for though..."

The young man reached for the handle and nudged the car door open with his foot.

"A couple more names please, 'Mr.Hunter'"

"Steve Hurst...and Neil Yardsley." He slammed the door closed, flicked his cigarette over the parapet and headed towards the stairwell door. As Barton turned the ignition and the Mondeo coughed into life, the young man in the Henri Lloyd coat turned to face the car.

"Make sure I get a tug as well. Questions will be asked otherwise."

Andy Barton nodded and smiled. "Maybe sleep in your best pyjamas for a few days eh?"

Chapter 2

"I'm glad you came. It means a lot." Max Jackson was suddenly aware that he and Rochelle hadn't spoken since they'd stopped at Trowell services on the northbound M1 nearly an hour earlier. It was only as the twelve-year-old VW Polo passed beneath the M62 flyover that he realised they were finally on the home straight.

"It's no problem." Her eyes remained fixed on the road ahead and he knew that despite her driving to Winchester Prison to collect him, there definitely was a problem.

Twenty one months inside had seen to that. He knew their relationship was over and she'd been seeing Steve's younger brother for a couple of months. He wasn't sure that she'd even come when he said his parole had been granted, and he was getting out fourteen months early. Non-Stop Nigel's death had clearly helped his case. Witnessing his old mate slowly dying of a heart attack in their cell, with the screws refusing to open the door, was something the authorities were clearly keen to hush up.

Her visits had become less frequent, 'car problems, no direct trains, no money', until he'd been lucky if he even received a letter every other week. It had been no surprise when she'd written to say said she'd moved in with Steve's brother. At least she'd kept the flat, which had given him an address to be released to.

He'd relived those crazy minutes next to the pier in Bournemouth so many times. Firing the gun was a stupid move but if he hadn't, would he, Nigel or Evrol still be alive? He'd spent every penny he had, and more, on a good brief who'd had the fingerprint evidence on the Glock dismissed as unsafe. Three years for affray had been a good result, but had wiped him out financially.

The news that Connolly's body had been found in the sea had been gleefully relayed to them by the West Yorkshire police who still were in Bournemouth on the Sunday morning.

"Great job lads. Your boss is dead. Aren't you meant to be his security?" Their laughter had echoed down the corridor, as Max and Nigel had contemplated life without Connolly. Even the worst case scenarios they'd discussed seemed better than the chaos Max had been reading about in letters sent from the lads back in Leeds.

'Drug Wars' screamed the headlines in the YEP clippings he'd received in the post. Shootings, revenge killings, kidnaps, and corpses in car boots had become regular subject matter for crime reporter David Bruce in recent months, as the city's gangs, plus their competitors from along the M62, jockeyed for position in filling the void left by the demise of Connolly's empire.

Max felt his stomach churn as he glanced left and saw the rows of red-brick terraces alongside the M621, which signified to every northbound Loiner that they were finally home. The three lanes snaked around to the right with the twin towers of West Riding House and City House dominating the skyline in the distance. Max told Rochelle to take the Holbeck exit just to see the 'Welcome to Leeds' floral display built into the Dewsbury Road flyover. No flowers today though, just a stray Morrisons trolley and an old tyre propped against the bare brickwork. Times were tough for the council, with thousands refusing to pay the new poll tax.

It would be quicker under the tunnel leading to the Scarborough Taps, but Max didn't object as Rochelle followed the road round to the right, past the new Asda headquarters, before swinging left past the Adelphi and over Leeds bridge. Then past the New Penny and Watson Cairns bike shop, where Max had once had a Saturday job, before he got sacked over some 'mates rates' transactions which never found their way into the till. Up Briggate, past the Harehills and Chapeltown bus stops next to the kebab shops. Familiar faces from Leeds 7 and 8, shuffling their feet, clutching market shopping bags and exhaling roll-up smoke, scanning the green and white double deckers, waiting in vain for a number 8.

"What will you do?" Rochelle turned and faced him as they waited at the red light opposite the Wrens.

"What do you mean?"

"What do you think I mean? For money Max. What will you do?"

"I don't have much choice, do I?"

She turned away as the lights changed.

"I'll go see the lads tomorrow. See what's what."

"For fuck's sake Max. You'll never learn will you?"

Rochelle shook her head and crunched the polo into third as they headed along North Street, LS2 turning into LS7, with Max hoping the bank of dark clouds forming over Scott Hall playing fields weren't a bad homecoming omen.

Chapter 3

Le Renard. The Dutchman knew it wouldn't be hard to spot him at the arrivals gate at Leeds Bradford airport. A 6'3, 10 stone beanpole, with a jagged scar running diagonally from the left of his forehead to his right ear would be instantly recognisable anyway, but it was the large tattoo of a fox's head on his neck which made him one of Northern Europe's most recognisable underworld figures. Le Renard, the fox. Some believed his nickname came from the tattoo, but others knew that it was actually the other way round. The tattoo reflected his character. Like a fox in a hen house, Le Renard just loved to kill, and when he started, he found it impossible to stop.

The Dutchman had been surprised when the Columbians had told him who'd taken the job. Five years ago, Le Renard would have been in New York or Rio, Shanghai or Moscow, exterminating political threats, avenging war crimes and settling criminal vendettas. Resolving mere hundred grand debts in northern English backwaters wasn't the sort of job Le Renard could be expected to entertain.

The Dutchman had made enquiries. It had taken a lot of calls. One mention of Le Renard had caused most of his contacts to hang up immediately. Slowly though, through whispered confidences and muttered anecdotes, he'd pieced together a picture of delusional psychosis, disturbing sexual deviation and prodigious drug abuse, which had caused Le Renard to disappear for almost a year. Now he was back on the books, and word was that he was eager to prove to the cartels that he was still the best in the business. A bomb in a Jakarta restaurant which took out twelve innocent diners as well as the politician it was intended for. A machine gun attack on a Milanese mobster's campervan on a lonely mountain road had put an end to his criminal career, as well as the lives of his wife, nanny and four young children. High profile jobs carried out with a level of violence which ensured they'd be analysed and discussed by the upper echelons of global criminality. Le Renard was back, and he wanted the right people to know.

"He loves to kill. Unhinged and unpredictable. Don't speak to him like you're his boss. Pity your enemies." The words of his contacts rang in the Dutchman's ears as the first passengers from the Paris flight began to emerge from beyond the frosted glass sliding doors.

The Dutchman looked around and grimaced, embarrassed by the tatty terminal building and smattering of poorly stocked retail outlets. Flying from Paris Charles De Gaulle to Yeadon Airport was likely to be a culture shock for the international assassin, and the Dutchman was left wondering why he'd accepted this particular job.

And suddenly there he was. Taller than the striding businessmen and shuffling elderly couples, yet less visible than the plump, city-break tourists in their matching shellsuits, searching the barrier for family members on taxi duty. Black leather jacket, faded stone washed jeans, dark hair, short and spiked on top, lank and collar length at the back. Face expressionless, scanning the waiting crowd, right eye pinched into a semi-wink where his scar crossed from eyebrow to cheek. Le Renard raised his head slightly and nodded in recognition as he spotted the Dutchman's raised finger.

"You speak English?" The Dutchman knew Le Renard was fluent in six languages, but it was an ice breaker. Not that it succeeded, as it yielded only a cursory nod in response.

Out through the sliding doors into a bright Yorkshire afternoon, across the car park to a soundtrack of a distant tannoy and the wheels of the Frenchman's wheelie trolley on the tarmac.

The smell of alcohol was overpowering as Le Renard got into the passenger seat of the Dutchman's car and pushed the seat back as far as it would go.

"They've booked you into the Hilton. It's probably the best hotel in town."

Another nod of the head. The Dutchman lit a cigarette and offered one to his passenger.

"I have my own."

The Dutchman took a left at the roundabout and headed towards the new underpass carrying the road beneath the runway.

"The Concord landed here a few years ago you know."

Not even a nod in response this time.

"It's a few miles into the centre. The Yorkshire Dales is a few miles in the other direction. Nice countryside. Have you heard of that?"

Le Renard sniffed and looked through the window at a queue outside a fish shop at the traffic lights.

"Tell me about the job," he muttered.

The Dutchman was sure he knew already. Everyone knew Le Renard researched any potential jobs thoroughly before accepting them.

"Low level gangster. Killed a couple of years ago while he was holding. Into the organisation for cash, drugs and guns. He'd been losing control for a while. Let people run up big debts and took his eye off the ball. Left a lot of loose ends."

"Two years? So why now?"

"That's a good question. When this guy died, we tried to pick up the pieces, but his firm had all been locked up over some crazy disturbance at a seaside resort in the south. We got to his main man, Jackson, inside, but the information he gave us was useless without local knowledge. Nicknames and vague addresses. No chance of us collecting. He's just got out, so the plan is to pay him a visit now. Take him along and collect what we're owed."

"How much?" Le Renard wound down the window and expelled a ball of phlegm as the car idled at Rawdon lights.

"What? How much are we owed? Maybe about a hundred."

Le Renard sniffed and shrugged. The Dutchman had to ask the question that had been eating away at him.

"It's a small amount for you, I guess. I know you've had much bigger jobs?"

No response from the passenger seat.

"I was very pleased when they said you were coming. But surprised also. If you don't mind me asking..?"

For the first time, Le Renard turned to face his driver.

"You want to know why I agreed to come here?"

"Well, I suppose you must have good reasons. It's not for me to know of course, if you don't want to..." the Dutchman worried that he'd overstepped the mark.

"There's someone here who I very much want to see. I hope to get to meet them while I'm in town."

The Dutchman detected a softening of tone and an almost wistful look in the previously hard, dead eyes of his passenger, which suggested a lost love. Maybe a childhood sweetheart, he guessed.

"This lady lives here? In Leeds?"

"Who said it's a woman?" The snapped response suggested to the Dutchman that he'd gone too far.

"And yes, he lives here. He has a job here. He's been here for a couple of months."

"That's great. Good that you can tie in a little pleasure with business eh? Does your friend know that you're going to be in town?" The Dutchman glanced left towards his passenger who was now silent again.

"He is expecting you, your friend?" The Dutchman smiled, eager to keep the awkward silence at bay.

No response initially, until Le Renard sighed and turned slowly towards him.

"Please stop talking now. You're starting to irritate me."

Horsforth slowly became Kirkstall, and to the Dutchman, the A65 seemed endless, as they crawled along in silence in the slow moving traffic approaching the viaduct. As the concrete clock tower of the YEP building appeared above the ring road flyover, a muffled snort prompted the Dutchman to look sidewards. Le Renard's eyes were closed, his mouth was half open and his breathing had slowed. Asleep, but his hands were still at work. Fingers straightening and contracting into fists, then extending one at a time as if counting. It was clear that for Le Renard, relaxation was an elusive ambition, and the Dutchman could only imagine the type of horrors which revisited such a man in his dreams.

Chapter 4

Tuesday 14 April 1992

Shot Soldier Dies - The hunt for three men who gunned down a soldier in Derby yesterday, became a murder inquiry today when the serviceman died. The Irish National Liberation Army has claimed responsibility for the attack.

"So you're confident these are the main Risk targets at the present time?" Chief Inspector Philip Holloway flicked through the loose-leaf A4 pages in the brown folder laying on his desk.

"That's the intelligence we've received sir." Andy Barton sat facing his boss and failed to conceal a grimace. A vigorous squash workout the previous evening had left him with a tweaked muscle in his lower back and he now struggled to retain his posture. Everyone knew Holloway was an old school stickler. Unpolished shoes, a crooked tie or slovenly gait weren't tolerated, whatever the rank of the offender.

"And it's reliable, this intelligence?" Holloway tilted his head back and peered down his glasses at the faces on the photos in the file.

"Of course sir. From an informant within the hooligan group itself."

Holloway removed his glasses and folded his arms, watching Barton squirm in his seat across the desk.

"An informant, yes that's right. Of course, you went against my suggestion of embedding some of your men within the group as covert surveillance sources. That's worked well for us before, and for other forces. I actually came up with the idea of the poacher in the Wild Boar operation you know..."

"Yes, I'm aware of that sir, but these groups are much more guarded following those previous operations. More organised, closer-knit. Very hard to penetrate..."

Philip Holloway stood up and walked to the window. He opened the slatted blinds and looked out across the stalls of Kirkgate's open market.

"This op needs to come off Andy. We need a trial, something that stays on the front page of the YEP for a few weeks. The Chief Super is asking questions about the funding that your unit has received since Bournemouth, why we've seen no tangible results."

"Sir, if I may...there have been no serious outbreaks of disorder since Bournemouth. Isolated incidents yes, but nothing that's hit the papers. Surely that shows that our strategy is working?" Andy Barton took the opportunity to stretch while his boss's back was turned and winced as his lumbar muscles extended painfully.

"Andy...you've been temporarily promoted to the rank of Inspector to head up the expanded football intelligence unit..." Holloway turned to face him again.

"Yes sir."

"You're now in a senior management position, so I think...I hope, that I'm in a position where I can level with you..."

"Of course sir."

Holloway turned away, his gaze following George Street up to the distant junction with Harewood Street, the first stallholders slipping across the road for an early lunchtime pint at the Mad House.

"Simply preventing disorder is fine Andy, providing it costs nothing to do that. The whole thing becomes a non-event. The public and media are untroubled by violence in the streets and stadia, and the force's budget isn't impacted. However, when costs are being incurred, and significant costs at that, for additional manpower, surveillance technology, your promotion...temporary promotion... there becomes an obvious imbalance....do you follow?"

"I think so sir..." Andy Barton nodded but his face betrayed the fact he clearly didn't.

"As far as the public, the media and the politicians are concerned, there is no football violence. It's disappeared, and therefore it's no longer a problem. They become more concerned with car crime, drugs and raves, and gang related murders in the streets of Chapeltown and Harehills."

"Yes sir..."

"But we're still spending a fortune on your team Andy! Blowing thousands on a problem which doesn't exist in the minds of the public. And from the perspective of the Chief Super and the ACC, that therefore represents wasted funding. Do you understand?" Holloway turned back to face the room, his hands resting on the windowsill.

"I do sir, yes I think I get it, but I'm not sure what you're suggesting...what's the solution? Surely we don't want disorder to occur just so it's seen as a problem by the public again?"

Philip Holloway sat down and smiled across the desk at Andy Barton.

"Andy, you're the expert here. As I said, you're now, temporarily, in a management position. You've always been good at problem solving. Now you have a different type of problem to solve..."

Holloway continued to smile across the desk and the ensuing silence was as unexpected as it was disconcerting to Andy Barton.

"I'm sorry sir, you've lost me. What are you asking me to do?"

The smile vanished quickly from Holloway's face, and he sighed deeply and loudly.

"Okay Andy...in the interests of time, I'll help by suggesting a number of potential scenarios which could play out here."

"I think that would be useful sir, thank you."

"Scenarios one and two are linked, in that they both seek to address what I'll term as our 'cost versus non-problem' equation. We have a cost, so we therefore need to establish a problem to be solved in the minds of the public and the media. Yes?" Holloway prodded at the brown file as he spoke.

"Erm yes, I think I so sir." Barton wriggled in his seat with his back locked in a painful spasm.

"One example of such a problem might be highly organised criminal firms, led by vicious hooligan generals with extreme right wing links, seeking to undermine the very fabric of society. These groups would need to be targeted via high profile, intelligence-led operations, a network of spies embedded in hooligan gangs, dawn raids on perpetrators etc..."

"Just as we're doing now sir." Barton felt confident that he was starting to catch up.

"Exactly Andy, exactly. However, if this strategy were to fail, we would obviously need to look at alternatives."

"Alternatives sir?...I'm not sure what those could be?"

"Back to our cost versus non-problem conundrum. Perhaps our problem could be the re-emergence of soccer violence in the media. Stadium riots, trains and pubs wrecked, running battles in city centres becoming front page tabloid news again. Just like the mid-eighties." Holloway's eyes flashed with something looking suspiciously like excitement to Andy Barton.

"But sir, we've done so much nationally, put so much work in, that would be a huge step backwards..."

"Quite...however..." Holloway stood again, his voice now raised. "The only other option, as I see it, is that we address the other side of the cost versus non-problem equation."

"Sir..?" Andy Barton was struggling to keep up again.

"There is no longer any problem, ergo, there should also be no cost. We disband the football intelligence unit, put the onus back on Holbeck handling any isolated matchday disorder as it arises, put your team back on the beat...and you go back to being a sergeant."

"I understand sir." The penny had finally dropped for Andy Barton.

"Good. So, let's hope your intelligence source has delivered. Go out, arrest the targets, make the charges stick and get them to trial. Then prepare for lots of press conferences Inspector...Acting Inspector." Philip Holloway extended his right hand, palm outstretched and showed Andy Barton the door.

Chapter 5

The Fforde Grene. A red-brick monstrosity of a pub with an apparently mis-spelled name. Max Jackson had grown up five minutes away in Karnac Road, so for him, the Fordy had always been there, dominating the corner where Roundhay Road hit the junctions of Easterly Road and Harehills Avenue. Now, seeing it for the first time in nearly two years, it seemed strangely out of place in Leeds 8, with wide chimney stacks and ostentatious gold lettering spelling out its name, said to have been derived from the 13th century manor house of a Tetley's director.

It had been a popular residential hotel when it was built back in the 1930's and then forty years later had reinvented itself as a music venue, playing host to emerging talent such as the Sex Pistols, Simple Minds and Dire Straits. Now its 'Man o'War' bar attracted only elderly West Indian dominoes players, minor drug dealers, and street hookers, whose numbers had recently increased when the police had finally closed down The Gaiety. It had also become a favoured meeting place for the ex-employees of Alan Connolly.

Max had put the word out amongst the boys, and there was a good turn out around a table in the far corner of the room, behind the pool table. The faces of Evrol and Steve, Fat Colin, Tom Brown the boxer, Luigi the mechanic and the twins Leroy and Mark were all visible through the ever present veil of smoke, as Max pushed opened the door and entered the bar.

If he'd been dreaming of a happy homecoming party while he was locked up, he was to be disappointed. The mood was subdued, defeated. The boys looked scared and tired.

"Sorry about Non-Stop Nigel mate. Must have been rough that." Evrol was the first to speak.

Max nodded and took a deep breath to reply but the words wouldn't come.

"And I'm sorry about Rochelle and our kid." Steve shook his head. "I had no idea man, and once I found out..."

"Don't worry mate. It's not a problem." Max lied, happy to shift the conversation away from Non-Stop's death.

"Got you a drink. Rum and coke still?" Evrol nodded towards a glass on the table and Max pulled up a stool and sat down.

"I've seen the press stuff you've been sending down. What the fuck's been going on?"

"It's war man. Total war." Steve shook his head and looked at his feet, and Evrol picked up the story.

"The boss getting topped happened at a bad time Max, the worst possible. Frankie Burns got out of nick two weeks later and it all kicked off. He shot Skinny Lance outside Sonny's Blues. Then a lad who was working for Lance took a couple in the legs outside Harvey's in town. Next, Frank had a go at Big Clinton, shot him three times, but Clint managed to drive himself to Jimmy's. They say he pulled one of the bullets out himself and handed it to the receptionist." The rest of the lads shook their heads and smiled in admiration, before Leroy picked up the tale after drawing on the last of his spliff and stubbing it on the table.

"For some reason, Clinton thought it was the Burley lads who'd tried to do him, and he sent a couple of his boys to do a drive-by outside the Hyde Park pub. Useless bastards missed though." More smirks and shaken heads.

"Then the Burley lads attacked The Masons in Lincoln Green one Sunday lunchtime. Axes, hammers, machetes, you name it. Clinton and his boys had been tipped off though, and ambushed them as soon as they came through the door.

"A Sunday dinnertime? That's a bit out of order." Max was beginning to get a sense of how out of control things had got.

"A right mess. Claret sprayed all over the carvery apparently." Evrol grinned a broad smile.

"Then Clinton turned up dead in' boot of a car near Potty Park a couple of weeks back."

"Who did that?" Max was struggling to keep up.

"No one knows mate. Rumours of a Manchester connection. People think it might have been them who did the gaffer too."

"Christ, that's all we need. So where do we fit in to all this now?"

The lads shifted uneasily in their seats and exchanged nervous glances.

"We were hoping you'd be able to tell us Max. As it stands, we're fucking nowhere." Evrol took a swig from his Guinness Foreign Extra bottle before continuing.

"We've still been running the weed from London on a very low-level basis, but to be honest we've all just been happy to keep our heads down. With everything that's going on, without Connolly, we'd be sitting ducks if we started moving any serious weight."

Max sipped his drink, and the only sounds were the crack of dominoes from two tables of pensioners in pork-pie hats at the other side of the room. He leant in towards the table and lowered his voice.

"I had a visitor when I was inside." He took another swig from his glass as the lads leaned in closer. "The Dutchman."

Steve exhaled loudly and the others began to shake their heads.

"Fuck, that's no good man. The boss owed him twenty five grand." Evrol had hoped for good news in the form of a plan, but things seemed to be getting worse.

"It was actually a lot more than that." Max clinked the ice in his glass.

"Ah for fuck's sake, we're dead. I knew it, we're all dead." Fat Colin was up and heading towards the toilet holding his head in his hands.

"Calm down Col, hear me out." Max shouted after him, but Colin was gone.

"The thing is, as you know, the boss wasn't the best record keeper. The accountant handled all that stuff, and the Dutchman knew that." Max threw down the last of his drink.

"Unfortunately, the accountant disappeared didn't he?" He looked at the row of blank faces across the table and smiled.

"Vanished without a trace didn't he? And all the records of who owed what to the gaffer have gone with him haven't they?"

"Yeah, but we know those two lads nicked the bag of cash, and the tyre shop bloke never paid for all those shooters..." Evrol was doing some mental calculations.

"And the boss always let Eddie No-Ears have too much on tick..." Leroy chipped in.

"Correct boys! And the best part of it is, it's all word of mouth. We only know all this because we were there. The Dutchman hasn't got a clue. I told him I didn't get involved in that side of the business and sent him off to look for the accountant."

"And he certainly won't find him. Not in one piece anyway." Steve smiled at the realisation that things might not be so bad after all. "Do you think he bought it though Max? Did the Dutchman believe you?"

"Well he never came back. And if he didn't believe me he'd have been sniffing around here, wouldn't he?"

A silence descended, broken by one of the pensioners slapping his domino down with a crack. All around the table pretended not to flinch, then seven pairs of eyes turned towards the door.

"Well, he definitely hasn't turned up here." Evrol leant back and took a swig from his Guinness bottle.

"Not yet anyway."

Chapter 6

Wednesday 15 April 1992

A new row erupted last night over 'Mad Cow' disease after a leading Leeds microbiologist warned the risk of humans catching it was 'frighteningly high'. Professor Richard Lacey said there is a 70% chance that large numbers of people will suffer from a 'Mad Cow' related disease in the next twenty years.

"Late night Derek?" Andy Barton caught the eye of the yawning constable in the Millgarth briefing room and gave him a knowing wink from the front of the strip-lit office. "Just think of the overtime eh?"

Barton grinned. A 5am roll call on a dark, unseasonably cold morning had caused more than a few grumbles amongst the assembled officers, but he'd felt the adrenaline buzz as soon as he'd woken at 3am. FIO's often said football intelligence work was like a drug. If that was true, then dawn raids were surely the purest, top-grade heroin.

The explosive thrill of kicking someone's front door in was the culmination of months of work. Poring over hours of video footage, putting in the hard yards gaining trust and winning confidences. Or as in this case, getting an informer to cough up some likely names.

They'd all been at it in the past, he knew that. All he needed was some half decent evidence. Diaries and phone books containing numbers of hooligan contacts around the country; press clippings, NF leaflets and terrace war photos taken on a pocket camera; Stanley knives and coshes.

Five teams hitting the targets simultaneously, dragging them out of bed in their undies, confused and shaken, their wives and kids terrified and crying. Today Andy Barton would remind them who still ran things at Elland Road.

"Did we hear back from Calendar, Snowy? Look North said they'd probably send a film crew to Slater's house as it's nearest the studio, but I never saw anything from YTV?" Barton paced at the front of the meeting room as the last officers entered, clutching cups of coffee.

"No, I heard nowt from them boss. YEP said they aren't sending a photographer either but they will cover it if we recover owt of interest."

"Fucks sake, what are they expecting us to find, Susie Lamplugh living in Hurst's shed?" Barton carried on smiling but he knew that without photos of some serious weaponry, today's raids would be lucky to merit a single column on page 5.

"Ok gentlemen...and lady, of course. Didn't see you there love." Barton nodded towards a lone WPC sitting amidst the ranks of sniggering officers.

"Welcome to Operation Hunter. Today we'll be carrying out a series of raids on the homes of suspected football hooligans across the city. You'll be operating in colour coded teams of five, as per the names on the noticeboard which you'll have seen when you arrived. Snowy... Sergeant White, will hand out an intelligence dossier on each subject, which you can familiarise yourselves with en-route. This details family circumstances, presence of minors in the property etc, prior convictions and propensity for violence. You've all been briefed on the sort of things we're looking for, so hopefully everything should be pretty straight forward. We hit the doors simultaneously at 6am. Questions?"

A single hand appeared in the centre of the room from a plump officer in his mid-twenties with a boyish face.

"Yes...?"

"PC Calvert sir."

"Of course, Calvert, what's your question constable?"

"I just wondered what the basis is for this morning's raids, inspector? If the suspects or their families ask, what should we say?"

"The basis? What do you mean by that?" Barton furrowed his brow and rubbed his chin as he leant back on the briefing room desk.

"Well, I was wondering, partly out of interest and partly because I like to know the type of offender we're dealing with, what these subjects have actually done?"

A silence descended on the room as Barton licked at his moustache and contemplated his response.

"What they've done? Well, they're football hooligans, so the type of thing they've done is arrange and participate in mass disorder at various locations around the country." Barton smiled and glanced round the room,

"Any other questions?"

"So..." the same officer sheepishly raised his hand again and Barton sighed audibly and looked expectantly towards him.

"So, we have evidence of that? If they ask?"

"They won't ask Calvert. They all know the score. It's a game, us versus them, and today we win."

"But we do though, don't we?" Calvert looked embarrassed as the officers around him shuffled and muttered.

"We do what?" Barton looked at his watch then folded his arms.

"Have evidence that they've been fighting at football matches?"

"We have intelligence, constable. Good intelligence, from a source within the hooligan risk group. It's your job to find the evidence. Is that okay for you?" Barton glared at Calvert and the officer nodded uncertainly.

"Right, lets move out. I will be travelling with Blue team to the Yardsley address in Garforth. Neil and I have some history going back a number of years, so I'm sure he'll be pleased to see me. This is an important operation so let's execute it safely and professionally. Good luck everyone."

The officers stood amidst a clatter of scraping chairs and hubbub of chatter. Andy Barton smiled and cracked his knuckles.

"Come on Snowy, let's go spoil some bastard's day before they've even got out of bed."

Chapter 7

"Must be a cracking firm to work for, right enough?" The young man was chatty, as all Irish barmen are. Normally Le Renard preferred the French style. Silent, aloof, borderline aggressive. Today though, sat in the cavernous and empty Harlequins bar, adjacent to the Queens hotel, nursing a pint of lager and a brandy chaser, he didn't mind the company.

"What's that? Cracking? What is cracking?"

"A cracking firm? A good company, that you work for, is it?"

Le Renard shrugged. "Why do you think so?"

"Well, you didn't like the Hilton, so they moved you to the Queens. Can't say fairer than that, so you can't."

The Frenchman nodded and allowed himself a half smile. It wasn't so much that he hadn't liked the Hilton, more that the Hilton hadn't liked him.

After checking in, the Dutchman had accompanied him to his room on the seventh floor, overlooking the railway lines snaking south from Leeds station. Le Renard checked that his standard requirements for the job had been delivered. The keys to a Renault 19 GTS-X rental car. A Glock 18 semi-automatic, the '86 model, and a lighter Glock 19 as back-up. A German issue Kampfmesser 2000 combat knife and shoulder holster. Nothing too dramatic for England. His usual weaponry shopping list had been pared back to the bare minimum.

He'd made up for that with his list of medicinal requirements. Twenty grams of the purest Colombian cocaine from his paymasters' production line. Speed to stay awake, propofol to sleep. Ecstasy for amusement, a litre of Pierre Ferrand cognac for relaxation. Once he was happy everything was in order, he'd dismissed the Dutchman's attempts to discuss the details of the job over a meal, saying he was tired and planned an early night.

Then he'd followed his normal routine in a new city. Directed by the concierge, he'd ended up in a corner bar next to a bridge, called the New Penny. Though quiet in the late afternoon, it had a pleasing lingering aura of sweat and cheap sex. It wasn't long before he was buying drinks for a sallow skinned youth with haunted eyes and a wispy moustache. The boy's expression betrayed the fact that he'd never before seen a fifty pound note, when Le Renard had thrust one into the top pocket of his denim jacket.

Back at the Hilton, the Frenchman had nonchalantly returned the concerned glare of the concierge as the lift doors had closed with a ping, and it hadn't been a surprise when, after twenty minutes, there'd been a knock at his room door. He'd enjoyed watching the uniformed doorman back away as he'd opened it, naked and clearly aroused.

"Yes. Everything is okay. There is no problem." He'd smiled and closed the door.

Two hours later the concierge was back, with the reception manager and a security guard, talking about a violent disturbance and threatening to call the police. Le Renard had clearly spent too long in Russia, where the hookers were happy to plumb any depths of depravity for the right price. The English were different. Discovering the unconscious youth, bound, gagged and blindfolded in the bathroom, the skinny, junkie, room-service whore had become hysterical and run naked from the room and screamed her way down the corridor to the lift. Le Renard had already packed his bags when he'd heard the knock on the door.

He'd seen the Queens in the city's central square as the Dutchman had negotiated the one-way system upon his arrival. An imposing eight-storey building of white Portland stone, now turned a soot-stained grey, it looked more suited to Berlin or Warsaw, the lair of corrupt party officials and their mistresses and gimps. Le Renard found its flamboyant yet down-at-heel character much more to his taste than the sterile sixties concrete of the Hilton.

"What line of work are you in then?" The smiling barman polished a pint glass and faced the tall, thin drinker leaning on his bar.

"Security. Solving problems. Maybe some negotiation. This type of thing." Le Renard finished his brandy and raised his glass for a refill.

"That's grand. Sounds more interesting than bar work. How do you get into that then?"

Le Renard nodded towards the bar to indicate where the replenished brandy glass should be placed.

"It's a long story really. A long journey. I found by accident that I had a talent for...such things."

"I hope you don't mind me saying, but I love that tattoo on your neck, the fox, that's amazing. You like foxes do you?" The barman grinned a cheeky smile.

"I got that in the army. The Legion." Le Renard ran his fingers across the vulpine features covering the left side of his neck.

"You were in the Foreign Legion? Wow...you must have had some crazy adventures. Is that where you got the...?" The young Irishman ran his finger across his face in a rough approximation of Le Renard's facial deformity.

"Yes, that's correct." The Frenchman picked up his pint and swilled down the remaining half. It seemed the subject was closed as the barman began to pull him a refill from the Labatts pump, but after lighting a cigarette he continued.

"Congo Brazzaville. You know it?"

"No, 'fraid not. I've only been to Spain once, that's all."

"It's a bad place. Dangerous." The Frenchman turned towards the raised voices of an arguing couple, laden with shopping bags, struggling through the bar doors.

"You got the scar in a battle there did you?" The young barman handed over the pint of lager.

"A battle yes? In a bar. A whore opened up my face with a cut throat razor." The Frenchman smiled as the barman's eyed widened and his mouth fell open. "I've been to many dangerous places. So many..."

The young Irishman waited, anticipating more, but Le Renard changed the subject.

"While I'm here, I hope to get to meet someone who is very important to me."

"Yeah? Someone from France?"

"Yes. From my hometown, Marseille. I need to speak to him. It's very important and is the real reason I took this job."

"You're meeting him in here then are you?"

"No, no. I am not in contact with him. I don't know where he lives, so I will have to go to his work." Le Renard balanced his cigarette on the overflowing ash tray and took a swig of his pint.

"Okay, he works in Leeds centre then?"

"Not too far, I don't think. You can tell me maybe. Do you like football? Leeds United?"

"Yeah, yeah of course. Loads of Leeds fans in Ireland where I come from. He works for Leeds then does he?"

"Yes. He is a player for them now. His name is Cantona. You know him?"

Chapter 8

"I can't go through this again Neil, I just can't. I lived through it once with Richard and now it's happening again." Julie Statham buried her tear-stained face in her hands and rocked slowly back and forth on the sofa. Neil Yardsley struggled to contain the anger rising inside him, knowing that would be the worst possible reaction.

"What's happening again? I don't know what you mean Julie."

"The lies. The secrets. We promised each other after Bournemouth, there would never be any secrets between us..."

"And there aren't. There are no secrets and no lies."

"So why did the bloody police nearly smash the door down to arrest you at 5 o'clock this morning?" Julie stood, her chest heaving with heavy sobs above her pregnant stomach.

"Honestly love, I don't know. I've no idea where they got my name. I promised you that I was through with all that and I am..."

"I've lived through it before Neil. Lived with Richard's gambling. Now I've got it again with you and bloody football."

"It's bollocks! Absolute bollocks. They started trying to pin summat on me that happened at Spurs, and I didn't even go. You know that, it was' weekend of Dave and Angie's wedding."

"So why? Why did they come here? Dragging you off in front of the neighbours, turning the house upside down. Jesus, I thought it was about..." Julie turned away and looked out of the window at her neat garden and the cul-de-sac beyond.

"I know what you thought it was about. I did too for a minute. I was relieved when I saw it was Barton and his mates, not CID." Neil approached and she flinched at his touch.

"And what if they'd found the gun? For God's sake, why didn't you get rid of it?"

"It's buried. It's safe. I will get shut of it. I just wanted to keep it in case any of Connolly's boys ever came sniffing around again."

"You need to get rid of it. I can't forget what happened in Bournemouth while we still have it. We're having a baby Neil. We need to move on..."

"We have. We have moved on. I promise you Julie, I've done nowt wrong at Leeds games. I'll even stop going if that's what you want. First though I need to see' rest of' lads so we can try and work out who's stitching us up, because someone definitely is."

"Please Neil, no secrets and no lies, that's all I ask."

Julie left the room with an over-shoulder look that reminded Neil of the first day they'd met, two years ago. His first day out of prison.

Chapter 9

Thursday 16 April 1992

Police Find City Murder Weapons- Weapons believed to have been used in the brutal slaying of two men at a house in Beeston have been recovered by detectives. Detective Superintendent Steve Hudson said that the investigation team were now following 'good lines' of enquiry but would not comment further.

"So you sorted out the problem with your accommodation? We're ready to start work now?" The Dutchman looked across towards the silent presence occupying his passenger seat.

"What is this place, some type of hotel?" Le Renard ignored the question and looked up at the red brick building with its apparently misspelt signage.

"Fforde Grene? What does this mean?"

"Not got a fucking clue man, but I'm led to believe it's where we're most likely to find Max Jackson on a Thursday afternoon. And he's the man with the answers." The Dutchman turned off the ignition and the two men exited the car.

They reached a wooden door painted burgundy, and the Dutchman patted the bulge in his jacket pocket.

"You're ready?" He licked his lips, his mouth dry.

"Of course." Le Renard seemed relaxed, treating the job as the low-level inconvenience it obviously represented to him. He pushed open the door and blinked through a thin film of tobacco smoke into the gloomy interior of a large room.

A table of elderly black men turned to look at the newcomers, then quickly refocused on the black tiles clutched tightly in their fists.

"Over there." The Dutchman nodded to the far side of the room, where five men seated at a small table were silently observing their entry.

"Hello Max, how are you?"

Even though he'd spent nearly two years in prison, Max Jackson's face seemed unnaturally pale, like he'd seen a ghost. He opened his mouth but no words came out and he simply nodded slowly in response to the Dutchman's question.

"This is my associate, Mister...erm..." He looked quizzically towards the tall man who was staring intently at each of the seated men in turn.

"Renard. They call me Renard."

"Mr.Renard has been sent by my employers to help us recover some of the funds and produce that your associate Mr.Connolly was in possession of when he met his unfortunate end."

"I told you when you came to see me, I don't know anything about that. The accountant and Mr.Connolly handled all that side of the business." Max was visibly shaking, as Evrol picked up his empty glass and rose from his seat, heading towards the bar.

"Sit down black boy." Le Renard's voice was calm and quiet, and he spoke without looking at Evrol, who immediately retook his seat.

"We spent several weeks trying to trace this accountant you mentioned, without success. No one had seen him for some time at any of the locations you suggested." The Dutchman picked up a yellow Castlemaine beermat and rotated it slowly between his fingers.

"It was suggested though, that you may have information which could help us recover some of our employer's possessions."

"No, I'm really sorry Mister...sorry, I don't know your name?"

"You don't need to." The Dutchman carried on revolving the beer mat.

"I'm sorry but I really don't know anything about who ended up with the stuff or where you can find it..."

"And that is why we have brought in Mr Renard." The Dutchman placed the beermat firmly on the table and leaned in towards Max.

"Mr Renard is the best in the business. He will help you trace the people who are holding things which don't belong to them, and he will...persuade them to pay back what is owed."

Max swallowed hard and looked around the table for support but found none. Evrol, Steve, Luigi and Leroy shifted silently in their seats and looked at the floor. The Dutchman pulled up a chair while Le Renard remained standing, his gaze fixed on Max.

"So, how about we begin with the low hanging fruit? These two boys who stole my cash. It seems to be fairly common knowledge around here that they're living in London." The Dutchman rested his elbows on the table and stared hard at Max.

"I've honestly got no idea. The last time I saw the one who stole the bag was when we all got arrested in Bournemouth. As far as I know, his case didn't even go to court. I haven't seen him since that night." Max's eyes darted from the Dutchman to the tall foreigner standing behind him.

"The rest of you...you have been around here since then. What have you heard? If we know about London, then I'm sure you do too." The Dutchman scanned the faces across the table, and Max caught Evrol's eye and a slightly raised eyebrow told him to share what he knew.

"I've heard they're living in Clapham. I honestly don't know where though, but I do know people who might."

"Okay. Good. You have until Saturday to find out. Also, I strongly suggest that between now and then, you will also remember everyone else who owed your boss money or was in possession of our produce." The Dutchman stood up and faced Max.

"And you. You will meet Mr. Renard here at 8am on Saturday. Don't be late. Mr. Renard will not be pleased if he has to go looking for you. You will go with him."

"Go where?" Max glanced at the tall foreigner then quickly looked away, unsettled by the dead eyes staring back at him.

"You will help him recover our property and funds. If you succeed you will be rewarded. We understand you're having a little local trouble here. We can help you with that. Get you re-established."

"But I told you, we don't know where the lads are. We don't know who owes what. I'm telling the truth."

The Dutchman turned to his companion and the tall man with the scarred face took a long inward inhalation and tilted his head to the right, displaying the sneering visage of the fox on his neck.

"I suggest then that you make some enquiries very quickly. You will meet me here on Saturday at eight and you will have the answers we need. Do you understand?"

Max nodded and felt his bowels liquify under the unblinking gaze of Le Renard.

"Good. On Saturday we go to London. Here at eight. You won't be late."

Chapter 10

Friday 17 April 1992

Souness Faces United - Graeme Souness, making a remarkable recovery from his triple heart by-pass, plans to have a big say as Leeds United and Manchester United continue to battle for the Championship. The Liverpool manager, still in hospital after his life saving operation, but deeply engrossed in team affairs, hopes to be fit enough to select the Liverpool side for the Easter Saturday clash with Leeds.

"That's the team bus going past now mate."

The landlord at the Old Peacock leant across the bar and gestured towards the window facing out onto Elland Road. The tall Frenchman stood, pint in hand and watched as the Wallace Arnold Gold Rider coach passed the pub car park.

"You don't need to drink up yet, they won't come out for about half an hour. The bus is late actually. They'll get caught in traffic on the '62 around Manchester setting off at this time, especially with it being Easter weekend."

The Frenchman watched the bus pass the rear of the stadium and made his way to the bar.

"So the match tomorrow is in Liverpool?"

"Yes mate. It's only 80 miles but Wilko likes them all in a hotel where he can keep an eye on them. Big game tomorrow an' all!"

"And I will see the team when they get on the bus?"

"Yeah course, no problem, just wait by the dressing room door. Watch out for old Jack though, he's a right miserable old twat."

"He is the team coach?"

"No is he bollocks, he's like the car park attendant. Wears a white peaked cap and a blazer though, so he feels important. Thinks he's in' army or summat."

Twenty minutes later, Jack Smith, ex Para and for the last ten years, car park manager at Elland Road stadium, was staring up into the face of the scowling, scar-faced man who stank of beer and sported a ridiculous fox head tattoo on his neck.

"You need to get back behind the barrier sir, I won't tell you again."

Le Renard glanced down with a look of mild annoyance, but maintained his position directly outside the players' entrance beneath the West Stand.

"Sir, I've asked you a number of times to move. Please get back behind the barrier." Jack slid his hand into the small of the Frenchman's back and applied a gentle pressure.

Le Renard had tolerated this petty official up to now, but laying a hand on him was a step too far. He span around and gripped the older man's shoulder and lowered his own face, until their noses were two inches apart.

"Don't ever fucking touch me," his breath smelled of beer and tobacco and chemicals, and made Jack recoil and stagger backwards, his cap askew on his head. He was well used to dealing with boisterous fans, and had clipped the ear of kids who got too close to the player's cars, and manhandled hooligans who threw coins at the directors' box windows. At sixty eight, he could still handle himself, but his years in the forces had attuned him to imminent danger, and this character exuded an unmistakable air of menace.

"Alright sir, there's no need for that language. I'm just doing my job. Please just step behind the barrier or the players won't be able to get past."

Le Renard recognised the familiar look of fear in the old man's eyes and took a couple of steps back, to stand alongside two autograph hunters in their mid-teens.

Behind him, a small, middle-aged man in a blue Umbro sweatshirt was supervising the coach driver and another man in loading crates of sporting equipment into the luggage compartment of the bus. The blue-painted, wooden door leading to the changing rooms swung slowly open and another balding, middle-aged man emerged, wearing an identical sweatshirt, bearing the initials MH on the left breast. The proximity to Eric's colleagues caused Le Renard's heartbeat to quicken.

"Stand back please." A couple of other bystanders had wandered over, and the man in the cap waved his arm towards them, but avoided making eye contact with the tall foreigner.

The door opened again, and a gangly black man emerged wearing a blue and yellow tracksuit top and carrying a small holdall. His head was dappled with bald patches, and as he passed, the smell of liniment transported Le Renard back to the Legion's boxing gym at Aubagne.

Next came a group, all wearing the same blue and yellow tracksuit uniform and led by a limping, stocky player on crutches. He was followed by a tall, dark haired young man with filmstar good-looks, and a grinning twenty-something with centre parted, lightly gelled hair, who shared a joke with the old man in the cap as he passed. They joined the others in climbing the steps onto the coach, with a couple of the players pausing to scrawl an autograph on a photo or book thrust at them by one of the teenagers, but no one looked at the Frenchman with the scarred face and the tattooed neck as they passed.

Le Renard inhaled and counted slowly in order to control his breathing. Eric was close now, he could sense his presence and his heart felt like it was about to explode from his chest. He'd rehearsed what he would say a hundred times, but now the moment was here, he began to worry that it was the wrong time and place. Too many people, not enough time to speak freely, to tell Eric his story.

The door opened again and a small man with ginger hair emerged, looking back while engaged in animated conversation with a tall, thin teammate with a long face and a receding hairline.

Following them, a man of around fifty, wearing the same tracksuit as the players, but holding a folder of papers with a transparent cover. Only he seemed to notice the tall stranger standing by the corner. Le Renard met his gaze and held it as he approached, and it seemed for a second that the man was about to speak, but as he drew level, he looked away. Le Renard watched him approach the door of the coach, and begin to climb the steps in slow motion. The sounds of the car park suddenly distorted, and his vision blurred, as a shock of adrenaline surged through his body. All his senses seemed to be in overdrive, and he knew Eric was close now. He turned to see the changing room door swinging open, and all too quickly, there he was. Taller than he'd remembered, but his posture, straight backed and barrel chested, was unmistakable.

A powerful wave of vertigo dizzied Le Renard and he had to grip the wall corner to steady himself. He could barely bring himself to look into those dark eyes, dancing mischievously beneath a thick mono-brow.

Dressed in the same blue and yellow tracksuit as the others, he held the door for a team mate to emerge behind him, tall and blond, smiling, chatting, holding his attention. Cantona was three paces away when his gaze met Le Renard's for an electrically charged split second, before he quickly turned away.

"Eric." The saliva seemed to have drained from his mouth, rendering the word inaudible. Cantona was level now, his face in profile and within touching distance across the barrier, tilting his head to remain attuned to the conversation of the man behind him.

"Eric...!" Breathless but louder this time, too loud in fact. So much so, that the blond haired man turned to look. In front of him, Cantona paused and glanced over his shoulder.

"Mon ami, C'est Pascal, d'Auxerre. Vous souvenez-vous de moi?" The tall stranger leant across the barrier, beaming a wide smile, his nostrils flaring as he inhaled the faint aroma of Tiger Balm and aftershave.

Cantona shrugged and smiled and shook his head. Then he raised his hand in a half wave and turned towards the bus.

"Eric...s'il vous plait. Je dois vous parlez!"

Le Renard had imagined this meeting in his mind a thousand times. He knew it was unlikely he'd be invited onto the team bus, it was Eric's place of work after all. It was far more likely that after he'd listened to Le Renard's story, Cantona would call out onto the bus and ask if anyone had a pen and paper. Then he'd note down his address and phone number. Tell Le Renard to call after the weekend so they could meet up and he could take the time to hear what Le Renard had to say. They'd talk about their lives while drinking a good bottle of Chateau Vignelaure. Perhaps Isabelle would cook them a bouillabaisse while they kicked a ball around the garden with Raphael. Then they'd eat, and sit and chat and laugh, swap memories of Marseille and Auxerre.

Only now, Eric wasn't asking for a pen and paper. He was striding towards the coach steps without looking back, and Le Renard was pushing the barrier aside and the old man in the hat was standing in front of him, raising an arm and blocking his way.

"I fucking told you...don't ever touch me!" Le Renard gripped the old man's shoulders and positioned his right heel just behind the man's calf. A light push was all that was required to send him spinning backwards, twisting awkwardly as he hit the ground. Jack Smith groaned in pain as his white hat came to rest beneath a blue barrier.

Le Renard turned to see Cantona climbing the steps of the coach and wheeled around to deliver a kick to the old man's face. With his victim curled into a ball at his feet, Le Renard tried to maintain his balance while fighting back tears of frustration. The body-slam which propelled him into the wall was delivered by a powerfully built black man with the boyish features of a young teenager.

"Calm down! Leave it! He's an old man. What's the matter with you?"

Le Renard heard a hydraulic hiss to his left as the coach door closed and then the changing room door opened with a bang, and two men in suits and more blue and yellow tracksuits spilled out, as someone shouted to call the police.

Le Renard felt the grip of a strong hand on his arm, but a glancing blow from his forehead onto the nose of his captor freed him, and he was off and running, under the huge floodlight pylons, following the oval of the ugly concrete stand. Through the gates and under a tunnel beneath a motorway. Panting as he ran, he glanced back to ensure he wasn't being followed, but the road through the industrial units was empty, and he realised the laughter echoing in his head was only the ghosts, blood soaked and vengeful as always, laughing at him for losing control again.

Reaching a railway bridge, he followed the direction of the train tracks and was still running when he arrived at the doors of the Queens Hotel. Into the lift and still gasping for breath when he reached his room, rummaging in his washbag for the cocaine and the ecstasy. A large brandy in his hand as he climbed into the shower to wash away the sweat and the tears, trying in vain to silence the laughter of the ghosts, echoing in his head.

An hour later and he was out, brushing past the bus queues and office workers heading home for the Bank Holiday weekend, his mind racing. Replaying the afternoon's events, his failure to tell Eric his story, which had caused a terrible darkness to descend, a darkness that he now bore like a heavy weight.

Turning right down the slope of Lower Briggate, Le Renard crossed the road towards the New Penny, his heart thumping and his mouth dry. A young man in a checked shirt with spiked hair stood in the doorway, a cigarette held between two fingers, smoke exhaled theatrically as he caught Le Renard's eye. The tall Frenchman stopped in the doorway and glanced back at the man, who looked away with a coy half smile.

Turning again, he walked away from the pub, feeling suddenly re-energised, like he was about to explode. He followed the bend of the road, past a pub on the right, 'The White Swan'. A drunken woman, heavily made up and middle-aged in her early thirties, swayed in the doorway. She raised her eyebrows as he approached. More sex. Was there nothing more for people to do in this fucking city than sell themselves?

He entered the pub with its long corridor and small rooms off to the left and right, a bank of payphones on the wall. The smells of cigarettes, stale beer and unwashed bodies from another day. It was quiet now with just a couple of lone drinkers staring at overflowing ashtrays, and an elderly couple with plastic supermarket bags silently staring at the bar. This wasn't the place to find what he needed, to quell the rage inside him, to stop his heart from thumping and his mind from racing. To appease the ghosts, give them the show they craved.

Up the road, attracted by the sound of music from a road on the right. Another pub. The Regent. Two large windows framing a central door, the dark interior busy, fat women staggering in front of the bar, dancing to Erasure's Respect. No one noticed Le Renard enter and take up position at the end of the counter, a pint of Lowenbrau and a glass of brandy alternately occupying his right hand, watching the citizens of Leeds welcoming the bank holiday weekend.

The women swayed and shrieked, the men grinned, glassy eyed, and shouted and prodded at each other's chests when they addressed each other. Le Renard observed and analysed. The drunkard, the hi-vis manual worker, the shop girl, the thief, the drug addict, the bully. The bully. He was the one. The one to release the tension and quieten the storm he knew was fast approaching.

Late twenties, tall and heavyset, a fat face with a pig's eyes squinting from beneath a checked baseball cap. Loose fitting, stonewashed jeans, Nike trainers and a blue jacket bearing a crocodile logo, he held court in the corner of the room. Legs spread wide, his face fixed in a perma-sneer, his acolytes grinned as he jabbed his finger towards two teenage youths cowering on an adjoining table. Le Renard couldn't hear what was being said above the pounding bass, as he observed the ritual posturing of the apex male. He smiled and felt his heartbeat begin to slow as the bully stood, arms outstretched, challenging the terrified youths. As usual, the supporting role in the pantomime was played by the bully's girlfriend, standing alongside him, pulling him back, imploring him to stand down. 'Leave it Steve, it's not worth it.'

The youths stood up, arms raised in submission, playing their part well. 'We don't want any trouble.' Half-finished pints left on the table as they backed away, heads down and making a swift exit, leaving the bully to revel in the attention from his group. His reputation was enhanced without even throwing a punch. Nutter, hardman, dangerous.

"Another drink love?" The barmaid with the badly bleached and permed hair tilted the empty glass towards Le Renard.

"No thank you. I think I'll be leaving very soon."

The Frenchman smiled as he gripped the spiked knuckle duster clenched in his fist and headed slowly and purposefully towards the bully in the corner.

The bully looked puzzled as he watched the tall stranger approach, and it was too late to take evasive action when he finally recognised the violent intent etched upon his face. He lost his right eye while still sitting in his seat. His jaw was broken as he scrambled desperately to escape from behind the drink-filled table, and his spleen was ruptured by the flying feet of his assailant as he curled in a ball in the corner of the room.

The electro-beat introduction of Rhythm is a Dancer pumped from the speaker, drowning out the hysterical screaming of the bully's girlfriend, as Le Renard paused to draw breath. His breathing felt calm and his heart rate had slowed, and most importantly, the ghosts had stopped laughing and now clapped their blood soaked hands, their cheers echoing in his head.

"Vive le Fin de Semaine! Long Live the weekend!"

Chapter 11

Saturday 18 April 1992

Serb Army Seizes New territory - Serb irregular forces seized new territory in fighting in the newly independent republic of Bosnia-Herzogovina, which UN envoy Cyrus Vance said was heading for disasaster. At least 100 people have been killed and 170,000 driven from their homes in a month of fighting over Bosnia's independence.

"Oh bollocks, he's here now. I can do without his moaning when I've got a hangover." Hursty grimaced as he blew the steam from his mug of coffee in the Bishopgate café at the bottom of Mill Hill.

Neil Yardsley turned to see Young Sutcliffe push open the café door, closely followed by Carl Elliot and Jamie Clifford. Sutcliffe nodded over to the table as he ordered two sausage and a bacon sandwich and three coffees.

"Didn't think we'd all be here today lads." Sutcliffe shook his head and pulled a chair up to the table as the new arrivals sat down.

"Me neither, and don't you think it's a bit strange that we are?" Neil took a bite of his bacon and egg sandwich and wiped egg yolk from his chin.

"They had nowt on anyone though did they? They had to give us all bail..."

"Yeah, but didn't you expect' bail conditions to say we had to stay away from grounds? They know we're off to Anfield today, they found' tickets when they searched Hursty's house."

"And a stash of porn mags that they showed to our lass." Hursty frowned as he took a sip of his coffee.

"So what are you thinking? Cheers love..." Sutcliffe leant back in his seat as the waitress placed a steaming mug on the table.

"I think they know they've got nowt on us, so they're going to keep letting us go to games, keep an eye on us and hope they can get summat on camera." Neil put his sandwich back on the plate.

"Well fuck that. I can't afford to get done. We've just bought a house." Carl shook his head and watched as an old man in a stained anorak waved a tea bag and tried to cadge a cup of boiled water from the waitress.

"Need to keep our heads down today lads." Hursty nodded his agreement.

"I've kept my fucking head down for the last two years but I still got nicked, didn't I?" Neil bit his lip and flashed a glance at each of the faces across the table, looking for clues but hoping not to find any.

"Barton that. Has to be. He's proper got it in for you." Young Sutcliffe met Neil's stare and held it.

"Nah, it's more than that. They kept talking about 'intelligence'. Someone's definitely feeding them information."

"Well they're not that intelligent are they? You weren't even at Spurs, and that's the one they kept asking me about." Hursty managed to raise a half smile.

"Me too. Kept asking who decided we should stay up at Kings Cross till half two. Said they knew it was me. I pissed myself. Said I didn't even know half the lads at' Duke of York so why would they listen to me?" Young

Sutcliffe lifted the top slice of bread from his newly arrived butty and grimaced at the barely cooked bacon.

"There's definitely a grass. There's a few lads been hanging around lately that I don't know. Jamie, who was that kid that was with us on' train down to Spurs, Wetherby Mark's mate?"

"I remember him, said he was from Skipton or somewhere out that way?" Hursty looked at Jamie too.

"Craig or summat? Weths used to work with him. What about him?"

"I didn't trust him. Summat strange about him. Kept popping up next to me all day, asking if I thought Spurs would turn up, then what do you know, they're outside and that smoke bomb comes flying through' pub door." Sutcliffe wrestled with the bacon rind in his teeth as he spoke.

"What, you think he was a Yid?" Jamie looked confused.

"No, you fucking idiot. I reckon it's him. He's either a copper or he's talking to Barton. Spurs couldn't have got there without' law knowing so they obviously let that happen for a reason."

"He's not a copper. Wetherby used to work on' railways with him. Always seems to have plenty of cash though. Maybe' coppers are paying him."

"I don't remember him being there for' Man U cup game though and' coppers seemed to know everything about that night." Hursty opened his wallet and removed two red match tickets, passing one to Neil.

"Yeah you're right. That's the one that worries me. Unless they're blagging, they knew we were all there that night. Either they were watching us on Gelderd Road when scum walked down from' Wheatsheaf or they're talking to someone who was there. And that's even more worrying. It could be anyone out of about fifty lads." Sutcliffe lit a cigarette and stared out of the steamed-up café window.

The table fell silent as they chewed on their food and revisited old suspicions and grudges, interrogating memories of lads who appeared and disappeared, popped up alone, a mate of a mate of a mate. 'Could be anyone out of fifty.'

Sandwiches were left uneaten on every plate, egg yolk congealing into bacon fat as Neil consulted his watch.

"Come on, its quarter to ten. Pick your butties up, we've a train to catch and a match to win. And we need to avoid bumping into any scousers. Heads down today boys!"

Chapter 12

"This is the place?"

"It's the address we've been given." Max Jackson looked up at the closed curtains of the terraced house in a quiet Clapham street, then across at the driver of the Renault 19. It had been a long morning.

The man he knew as Le Renard was already waiting when he'd arrived in the Fforde Grene car park at 7.45. He'd seemed jittery and excitable, and the cause of that was revealed when he'd dipped a Queen's Hotel room key into a large bag of white powder, and noisily inhaled it while hurtling towards the Wakefield junction of the M1.

Max had offered to drive when the Frenchman mentioned not having slept for two days, but his offer had been answered with a shaken head and a scowl. They'd then driven south at speeds which rarely fell below 95mph, with the hotel room key regularly dipped into the bag of powder.

"Did you learn English at school? I'd love to be able to speak another language."

"Do you always work in England then or...?"

"Are you married? I guess not..."

Max's questions had prompted neither a reply nor any facial response, as Le Renard gripped the steering wheel and stared at the fast-lane head, grinding his jaw and breathing loudly through flared nostrils.

The soundtrack for the three hour journey was a Depeche Mode mix cassette which culminated in

'Personal Jesus' and 'See You' being continually repeated for thirty minutes, with the tape ejected and flipped repeatedly at the end of each song.

"Are these your favourite tracks then?" Max had ventured nervously, with his question initially ignored for five silent minutes until the Frenchman suddenly responded.

"I enjoy songs with a meaning... like, this song says, you know I will deliver, because I'm a forgiver. What does that mean? Who is he forgiving and why? What is the delivery? Fuck man, I wish I understood, you know?"

Max had shrugged uncertainly and wished he hadn't asked. He'd also decided not to enquire about the bloodstains on Le Renard's jeans and his scabbed, swollen knuckles. It seemed that a quiet night before a job wasn't the Frenchman's style.

"Shall we go?" Le Renard was already exiting the car, scanning the street and the windows of the house.

"First floor, yes?" He removed a screwdriver from his pocket and fumbled with the lock as Max stood watch.

"I think it's better if I do the talking, I know them." Max whispered over his shoulder as they quietly climbed the creaking wooden stairs to the first floor landing. Le Renard shrugged his agreement.

"This one, flat 4." Max nodded at a mahogany door with a brass number plate, and Le Renard stepped forward with the screwdriver. Within thirty seconds they were in the hallway of the flat. A mountain bike was propped against a radiator on the left and a haphazard pile of shoes and trainers stretched towards a door on the right. The faint sound of snoring indicated that the room was occupied. Max crept along the corridor, passing another door to arrive in an open-plan kitchen and living room. A circular wooden table contained the silver tray remnants of a Chinese take away, five empty stella cans, a bag of heart shaped pills, an overflowing ashtray and an assortment of CDs and tapes. A long settee filled the far corner of the room, opposite a fat silver television and stereo system. A large black speaker filled the other corner next to the bay window.

Max nodded back towards the hallway and Le Renard turned and led the way to the first bedroom. Max spotted the gun in the Frenchman's right hand as he turned the door handle with his left. The creak of the door hinges prompted a muffled snort from the darkness of the room.

"Time is it?"

Neither Max nor Le Renard spoke.

"Time is it Danno? I feel fucked. What time did you..."

Stuart Yardsley flicked on a bedside table lamp and rubbed at his eyes.

"Afternoon mate. Long time, no see." Max smiled at him from the end of the bed.

Stuart blinked and tried to catch his breath. He'd thought about this moment every day for the last two years, and had countless nightmares about it, but now it had arrived, the excesses of the previous night seemed to have robbed his body of its fight or flight response. He slowly pulled himself upright.

"Max...I knew you'd come. I didn't know you were out."

"Last week. Have you missed me?"

Stuart's adrenaline now began to kick in, and he felt a sudden nausea rising as he looked up at Max's smirking face and the tall, impassive man with a scarred face and tattooed neck standing beside him.

"I had nowt to do with Connolly. You know that, I was in' nick all night, same as you."

"Yeah, but they dropped all' charges against you. I didn't get out for another two fucking years because of you and your mates. Poor old Non-Stop didn't get out at all."

"What can I say? I'm sorry, I fucked the whole thing up."

Max found himself laughing ironically at the kid's simplistic view of a situation which had virtually destroyed his life.

"And you think that's it? The end of it?"

"I don't know what else I can say. Can I get out of bed?" Stuart felt vulnerable lying naked beneath the duvet and swung his legs onto the floor.

"We've come for the cash." Max wasn't smiling anymore.

Stuart shrugged. "It's all gone. I'm sorry."

"Gone? What, you've gone through twenty five grand?" For Stuart's sake, Max hoped he was blagging.

"I paid for my mam to go to Australia. She died last year, but at least she got to spend her last six months with her sister somewhere that wasn't fucking Holbeck."

"Did you fly her body back on Concorde?"

"What?"

"Twenty five grand?"

"Yeah, she wasn't insured so we had to pay for all that, it cost a fortune..."

"Twenty five grand though?" Max was beginning to lose patience. The tall man accompanying him maintained his impassive expression.

"I paid for some decks that me and Danno use for work, and the deposit for this place. There's nowt left, honestly. I can pay you back a bit a month..."

Before Max could answer, the door opened behind them, and Mark Daniels appeared in his boxer shorts, rubbing his eyes.

"Stu, what the...Oh fucking hell."

Danno seemed to raise his right hand towards his face just before the sharp crack of the Glock echoed around the bedroom. His eyes registered confusion, then panic, in the split second it took him to retract his hand and find part of his lower jaw resting in his palm. He tried in vain to speak, as a jet of crimson sprayed the wall on his left, and within seconds he was slumped forward, resting on his knees, his throat rattling loudly as he drowned in his own blood.

Stuart roared in distress and leapt to his feet. Terror stricken, he retreated to the corner of the room, where he began to claw frantically at the wall, his blind panic overcoming the rational conclusion that there was no way out.

"What...what...what the fuck did you just do?" Max turned to Le Renard who was silently observing Danno's twitching body. The Frenchman ignored Max and took two steps to the centre of the room, raised the Glock and blew away the top of Stuart's skull. The naked corpse slumped forward against the wall, legs splayed out behind in an expanding pool of blood, as brain matter dripped from the bedside lamp.

"Jesus Christ. What the fuck...why?" Max had assumed an involuntary crouching position, his hands over his head.

"It's clear there is no money here. Why would we allow them to live?" Le Renard walked to the window and pulled back the curtains, checking that there was no activity in the street.

"These are flats. What about the neighbours?" Max was standing now, shaking violently.

"If they come, then we'll kill them." Le Renard moved across the room to flick the electric kettle on, then opened a kitchen cupboard to withdraw a cup.

"You want coffee?"

"No, I don't want fucking coffee, I want to get out of here. I've only been out of' nick for a week for fuck's sake!"

"What is nick?" Le Renard removed a polythene bag from his pocket, dipped his Queen's Hotel key in, and hoovered up a pile of powder.

"Jesus Chris, we need to get out of here." Max peered out of the window as Le Renard spooned some instant coffee into a cup and opened the fridge, sniffing a carton of milk and screwing up his nose. He then opened a drawer and produced a biro. Walking to the table he lifted a carton of rice to retrieve the brown paper bag which had contained the take-away. Max was bent over Stuart's body, trying not to retch, when he felt a tap on his shoulder and turned to see Le Renard holding the pen and bag out towards him.

"Write. The other names and addresses."

"What?" Max kept his hands by his sides.

"The others, who owe the organisation."

"I don't need to write it down. I know them, I know where to go..."

"Just write." Le Renard pushed the pen and paper towards Max, his tone making it clear that refusing wasn't an option.

"What's the point? It's not easy. I don't know proper addresses, you need to know where to go."

"Write, all the details. And make sure I can read it."

Max began to print names, volumes and amounts, addresses and descriptions on the brown paper bag.

"Fucking stupid, what's the point?"

But Max Jackson knew the point. Understood the plan now. Knew he would be found in a flat in Clapham with a single bullet wound to the temple. Knew the Glock 18 which killed him would also have been used to dispatch the two bodies beside him, and that the weapon would be found in his hand. A murder suicide. Open and shut case.

Max put the pen down and looked up into the eyes of Le Renard, who, for the first time since they'd met was smiling. Smiling as he raised the gun and positioned it just above Max's right ear, smiling as he said 'Au revoir,' laughing as he pulled the trigger.

Chapter 13

Monday 20 April 1992

Wharton Boosts World Claim – Battling Yorkshireman Henry Wharton has stepped up his claim for a world title fight later this year after emerging triumphant from his savage bout with Australian Rod Carr at a packed Leeds Town Hall. Leeds born Wharton is now virtually guaranteed a tilt at WBO champion Mauro Galvano's crown before the end of the year.

"So you had a good day out then love?" Neil Yardsley was in a buoyant mood as he retrieved a bottle of Budweiser from the fridge and joined Julie on the couch.

"Yeah, we went to that new Tropical World place at Roundhay Park. It's just like a big greenhouse really, but they've got a café and there's butterflies and stuff like that. My Aunty June liked it and it was nice to see her and catch up. Good match?"

"Not brilliant but we got the result. The sending off and penalty changed the game, thank God. We knew before kick-off that Scum had lost at home to Forest and it would have been just like Leeds to blow it. We're a point ahead now but they've still got a game in hand."

"No trouble?"

"It was Coventry at home." Neil tried to hide his irritation.

"What's that mean?"

"It means no Julie, there was no trouble, and as you know, even if there was, I wouldn't be anywhere near it!"

He shook his head and she picked up the TV remote and changed the channel. A young Sean Connery moodily brandished a spear gun in Thunderball, as Neil took a swig from the bottle.

"Jesus. Is this the best they can come up with on a Bank Holiday Monday night? ...Anyway, what do you think about Eric if it's a boy?"

"Eric? Yeah right..."

"He came on and won the penalty today. Strachan put it away...Gordon's not a bad name either, come to think about it." Neil ducked to avoid a cushion aimed at his head, as a car swung around the cul-de-sac then disappeared behind next door's hedge, before advancing slowly and drawing to a halt in front of their drive

"Who's this I wonder?" Julie craned her neck to get a better view of the occupants, but Neil already knew. The tell-tale second aerial on the roof of the navy blue Cavalier had already alerted him to the fact that, for the second time in a week, West Yorkshire Police were paying him a visit. He stood up and watched as Andy Barton climbed from the driver's seat, still sporting the brown suede jacket and white Nike trainers he'd been wearing when he'd done his town pub rounds earlier that day. An older man in a crumpled suit, heavier and balding, slowly emerged from the passenger side door. It was the occupant of the rear seat who caused Neil's heart rate to quicken though. A uniformed policewoman, late teens, retrieving her hat and straightening it on her head as they approached the drive.

"You wait here. I'll deal with this." Neil motioned Julie to remain in her seat, as her face fell, upon seeing the WPC's uniform.

The officers were halfway down the drive when Neil opened the door.

"What the fuck do you want?" He addressed Barton who was leading the expressionless threesome.

"Hello Neil...erm, is it okay if we come in for a word?" This was a different officer to the one who'd hammered on his door at dawn a few days earlier, and as Barton raised his hands in a gesture of submission, it was clear to Neil that this wasn't another raid.

"What's up...what is it?" Neil was panicking now, as the man in the suit and the young female officer avoided eye contact with him.

"Come on mate, let's go inside..." The fact that Andy Barton called him 'mate' caused a wave of panic to rise inside Neil.

"What is it? What's the matter?" Julie appeared behind him in the doorway.

"Mrs Statham...Julie...do you mind if we come in?" Barton was on the step now, his arm slowly guiding Neil back towards the living room.

"It's our kid isn't it? It's Stu...what's happened?"

It was now Andy Barton's turn to avoid eye contact.

"This is DS Milligan from CID and WPC Hollings...shall we go in and sit down?"

"Just tell me...tell me what's happened?" Neil was pacing the room, clutching his head in his hands as the young female constable ushered Julie towards the kitchen.

"My boss thought, as we...erm, have known each other for a few years, that erm, I would be the best person to come and see you..."

Neil stood opposite Andy Barton with his back to the gas fire, as the detective in the suit picked up the TV control and turned down the Bond film. Neil's chest was heaving and he could feel tears beginning to sting his eyes.

"Just tell me...please, what's happened..."

Barton took a deep breath. "I'm sorry to tell you Neil, that the bodies of three men were found this morning at a flat in Clapham..."

Neil had already sunk to his knees, sobbing loudly, as Andy Barton swallowed hard and continued.

"One of the deceased was your brother Stuart Yardsley. I'm really sorry Neil. I didn't know him well, but I understand he was a good lad..."

Julie emerged from the kitchen and crouched to embrace her distraught partner.

"I've put the kettle on." WPC Hollings whispered from the doorway as Barton and Milligan exchanged glances.

"How did he die?" Julie looked up while continuing to embrace Neil, who was now curled into a sobbing, foetal ball in front of the fire.

The two officers exchanged glances and Milligan nodded.

"The information we've received from London is that all three men died from gunshot wounds."

Julie's mouth fell open and Neil lifted his head.

"Gunshot...not drugs? You're sure?"

Barton nodded and Julie stood up, clutching at her mouth.

"Excuse me...I need to..." She dashed towards the kitchen, retching, as orange vomit spilled through her fingers.

"Fucking hell no... who...who were the others?" Neil knelt in front of the officers, gazing upwards like a child pleading for mercy.

Again, glances were exchanged between the officers. Milligan shrugged.

"Their next-of-kins may not have been informed yet, so I shouldn't really disclose, but I can tell you that one was his friend, Mark Daniels."

"Oh not Danno too. Fucking hell...why...why Stu?" Neil covered his face and rocked, sobbing, as the officers shifted uneasily in front of him. From the kitchen came the sounds of WPC Hollings encouraging Julie to drink water and asking her where the mop was kept.

"It's obviously a lot to take in now, but we will need to you to come down to Millgarth as soon as possible to make a statement. We'll let you know about identifying the body, and when you can gain access to the flat. WPC Hollings will stay for as long as you need tonight..."

Neil remained in his position on the floor as Milligan nodded towards the door and they turned to leave.

"His partner has taken it really badly. Must have been very close to the brother." WPC Hollings whispered as the officers shuffled towards the front door, then turned as she sensed Neil behind her.

"Thanks, but we don't need anyone with us."

"Are you sure Neil? You've had a big shock. Julie seems really upset too..." Barton turned and stepped back towards him.

"We've had enough police in this house over the last week don't you think? We just want to be left alone please."

Barton nodded and reached out to awkwardly pat Neil's arm.

"Yeah. No hard feelings on that eh? I'm just doing my job. If I don't do it, someone else will."

Neil couldn't be bothered to argue and looked down, shaking his head and watching tears fall onto the carpet.

Barton looked through the open door as his colleagues headed up the drive then turned to face Neil, lowering his voice.

"The other deceased male in the flat..."

Neil looked up.

"Someone we know. Max Jackson."

"Jackson? I'm not sure...?" Neil shook his head.

"Alan Connolly's right hand man."

The mention of Connolly hit Neil like a blow to the gut, and Julie's violent reaction to the news suddenly made sense. He'd assumed it was a drug deal gone wrong or a feud linked to the London club scene. Instead, his worst nightmare was coming true. The events of Bournemouth 90 were coming back to haunt them.

"He got out of jail last week for the Bournemouth thing. We couldn't pin the gun on him but he went down for affray and served nearly two years. The Met are saying it looks like a murder suicide. He killed the lads then topped himself. CID will want to speak to you about Stuart's links to Connolly, so I thought I'd give you the heads up. Remember, I've said nowt though..." Barton winked and turned to step through the front door.

"Yeah, I understand. Thanks for telling me." Neil closed the door and turned to see Julie emerge from the kitchen, her jumper spattered in vomit, and an angry, red, nervous rash spreading up her neck and across her tear-stained face.

"They know don't they, Connolly's friends know what I did?" She began to shake visibly and sob loudly and Neil tried to calm her, but couldn't find the words.

"It's my fault Neil. They've killed Stuart and now they'll be coming for us." Julie slid down the wall and huddled on the floor with her arms wrapped around her pregnant belly.

"Jackson's dead though. He killed himself. Maybe it was revenge for Stu getting him sent down, I don't know...it doesn't make any sense."

"Well, we need to find out Neil. Need to understand what's going on. There are others and they've come into this house once before, and I'm not going to just sit here waiting for them to come again."

Neil crouched next to Julie and wrapped his arms around her, as they listened to the tyres of the Cavalier crunch on the asphalt, as it negotiated the curve of the street and headed for the A63.

"I wasn't here last time was I? I am now. I'll sort it, I promise. I'll find out what's going on, and if we have to, we'll just disappear."

"But you can't find out can you? How can you ask the police if we're in danger without telling them about Bournemouth? I knew this wasn't over Neil, I knew it would come back and ruin everything." Julie sobbed and buried her face in her hands.

"I'll find out, but not off the police."

He stood up and looked down the hallway and out through the kitchen window. To the back garden with its wooden shed, rotary drier and small patch of grass, beneath which lay the remains of Marmaduke the cat, and a rusty tin box containing Scouse John's gun, which he'd buried forever two years earlier.

"I'm not sure how, but I'll find out what happened and why. Not just for us either, I need to find out for Stu."

Chapter 14

Tuesday 21 April 1992

Europe here we come! -Leeds United made certain of a place in the UEFA Cup when they beat Coventry at Elland Road yesterday, but they would go into the top club tournament- the European Cup- if they went on to clinch the First Division championship. That would potentially net the club a huge cash bonus of between £2m and £4m due to revenues from television rights and advertising.

"You've been busy." The Dutchman looked at the handwritten list he'd been given.

"What did you expect? I'm very good at my job." Le Renard lay naked on the double bed in his hotel room and lit a cigarette. "Your stuff is in the bathroom. Cash, guns, drugs. It's all there, in the bath. Two more collections to make. They needed time to get it together, but they will, don't worry."

"Max Jackson has been helpful?"

"Initially, he served his purpose, but I found him an annoyance, so I dismissed him."

"Dismissed him? Okay...and the names with the crosses?" The Dutchman looked from the list across to the bed.

"Those people are all dead."

"Dead?"

Le Renard shrugged.

"You mean they were already dead by the time you called on them...or..?"

Le Renard shook his head and furrowed his brow. "They were unwilling to help me...so...they're dead."

The Dutchman flinched and nodded. The stories about Le Renard were clearly true and he had no desire to remain in the man's company for any longer than was necessary.

"What will you do when you've made the final collections, go home?"

"Home?" Le Renard exhaled smoke and shook his head. "Where is home, do you think?"

"I don't know, I assumed you live in France."

Le Renard ignored the question and contemplated the long thread of ash threatening to spill onto the duvet. Feeling his attempts at conversation had overstepped the boundaries of privacy, the Dutchman quickly changed the subject.

"Did you manage to meet your friend?"

"He isn't my friend, just someone who played an important role in my life. I haven't managed to meet him yet. But I will. I have to." Le Renard swung his legs from the bed and walked to the window with the cigarette extending from the corner of his mouth. He tugged the net curtain aside and looked out at the line of black and white taxis snaking from the station and heading out along Wellington Street.

"You believe in fate?" He turned to face the Dutchman.

"Perhaps, I don't know for sure. Why?"

"I never believed in such things, but when I was contacted about this job, I thought maybe...?"

The Dutchman remained silent but raised his eyebrows to indicate his interest, and the Frenchman began to tell his story.

"Ten years ago, I was living in Auxerre. I'd had some trouble back in Marseille, jail then a mental institution. The police hated me, so a friend had got me a job in a bar there. I was also doing some small jobs for a local gangster. Driving, collecting debts and the like, trying to survive but I didn't really know anyone there." Le Renard signalled towards an open packet of cigarettes resting on the room's small desk, and the Dutchman took one from the packet and lit it.

"There was a gang of young guys from the Auxerre football club who used to come and hang out at the bar. Eric was one of them."

"Eric is the person who you hope to meet here?" The Dutchman narrowed his eyes in response to the harsh nicotine hit from the French cigarette.

Le Renard nodded. "I found out he was from the same part of Marseille as me. To me, it felt like we were brothers. Both young men forced to move away from our hometown with no friends or family nearby and I felt a connection to him immediately. I started to follow his career even when he was in the second team at Auxerre. I read all his match reports, went to the games to see him play, sometimes I'd even get to speak to him in the bar. The more I learnt about him, the more I knew that we were the same. Rebels who hated taking orders from idiots. Though he didn't know me, I felt connected to him, like what you'd call maybe a telepathy?" Le Renard paused and the Dutchman realised he was seeking affirmation, so nodded uncertainly.

"I was a few years older, so I tried to watch out for him, without his knowledge of course. Anyway, there was a gang of Moroccans, older kids, third rate street gangsters. They used to hang around the bar, and I got a bad feeling about them. I could tell they didn't like Eric because he was popular with the other kids. They spoke about him behind his back. They were jealous of him, and I became convinced they were going to try to injure him, end his career. He didn't know anything about it, but I decided that he needed my help, and as I was his biggest fan, I had to be there for him." Le Renard scratched hard at his naked crotch and his black eyes stared at the Dutchman.

"You fixed it with these Moroccans then?" The Dutchman stammered, suppressing an urge to check how far away he was from the room door, as Le Renard now paced manically in front of him.

"I tried but they just laughed when I warned them off. As I said, I was just a kid myself, maybe twenty, twenty-one years old. I was a nobody. They told me to fuck off and said they had no problem with Eric. I knew they were lying though, and I had to do something. I heard there was a guy in Appoigny, an Algerian, causing problems for my boss. Running a lot of hash, attracting too much police attention. I offered to do the job, take him out. They asked if I'd done that sort of thing before. I said of course, many times in Marseille."

"And had you? Killed someone?"

77

"No. Nothing like that. Anyway, they asked how much I wanted, and I said nothing. All I asked was that they fix the Moroccan problem for Eric, warn them off."

"So he was your first kill, this Algerian?"

"I stabbed him in the throat with some scissors while he was drunk. A messy job, I made a lot of mistakes. It wasn't long before our source in the police told me that my name was top of the list of suspects. That's when I joined the Legion. I heard that Eric was sent on loan to Martigues, and I never saw him again." Le Renard sucked on his cigarette and gazed out of the window.

"So it's a long time ...you've had no contact with Eric since Auxerre?"

"No nothing. He has moved around a lot as I have, but I never stopped thinking about him, I always followed his career. I still felt the connection, and when I heard about this job, I thought it was meant to happen, that fate had brought our paths together again." Le Renard put out his cigarette and immediately lit another.

"Loric Abrashi." His face remained impassive as he looked at the Dutchman for a reaction.

"The Lumberjack. Albanian. Killed a couple of years ago wasn't he?"

"Three years. 1989. I killed him in Milan."

"Yes I remember now...so that was you." The Dutchman had already guessed.

"I made a mistake in taking that job. I broke my golden rule. Never kill a fucking Albanian. Once you start, it never ends. Their family will not rest until they avenge the death."

"They came after you?"

Le Renard turned back to face the window. "I'm not an easy man to find, unfortunately."

"Unfortunately? Surely they would have killed you in a terrible way..."

"They would have done to me what I did to Abrashi, but they couldn't find me. They did find my mother and my sister though."

"Oh..." The Dutchman was glad Le Renard was facing away from him. He didn't want to see his face.

"I disembowelled him in the bath of his hotel room. Opened up his chest from his cock to his throat with an electric saw. Can you imagine?"

"I can't...I'm sorry." The Dutchman felt his breathing quicken and fought the urge to run.

"They cut the baby from my sister's stomach. Left it to die on the kitchen floor. I saw the police photos from my mother's house." Le Renard turned back to the Dutchman, his face betraying no emotion, his eyes dead.

"After that, the nightmares started. Nightmares I have whether I'm awake or asleep. The same blood that I saw on those photos, covering every surface of that same kitchen, but always different faces on the bodies. So many faces. So many ghosts, I can never escape them. They are always with me, making me question this path I've taken. Making me wonder where it all started to go wrong, to re-assess my life. You understand?"

"And Auxerre was the start of it?"

"Exactly! Le Renard was now pacing the room again, jabbing an index finger skywards.

"I set out on this path in Auxerre, to help Eric, to save his career. That path has led me in the wrong direction, to the darkest place. I understand that now, but maybe it was all still worth it, if some good has come from what I did."

"You mean saving Eric and allowing him to take the path he has, to become a big star?"

"Exactement!" Le Renard stopped, his face now inches from the Dutchman's, into which he exhaled smoke as he spoke.

"I must meet Eric to know the man he has become today. Then I will understand that it was meant to be, that I sacrificed my life for a greater cause, to create an amazing man, a hero, maybe even a Messiah. And when I tell him my story, explain what I did for him, he will tell me that he is grateful for that, that he owes me everything. He will lead me from the darkness into the light and maybe then I can accept this person that I've become. Perhaps then the ghosts will finally leave me alone."

The Dutchman nodded, but felt the need to turn away under the weight of the Frenchman's dead eyed-stare, which caused him to shiver involuntarily.

'Pity your enemies,' he'd been told, and clearly the margin between friend and foe was a very slim one for a man like Le Renard.

He hoped that the meeting the Frenchman so badly craved was destined to be a happy one, for everyone's sake.

Chapter 15

"So it's you then, you're here. I knew you'd come back."

The voice from the gloomy interior of the Strega 'nightscene' surprised Neil Yardsley almost as soon as he'd descended the tight stairway, and passed the metal cage which served as an entrance booth.

He extended his arm, Scouse John's gun just visible in the inky blackness, pointing it towards the voice.

"Please man, don't shoot me, I beg you, I've got kids." Neil could see the shape of a man moving slowly as his eyes grew more accustomed to the dark.

"Stay still and I won't shoot." Neil edged backwards, trying to feel for a wall, to ensure no one could approach him unseen from the rear.

"Okay man, I'm still. Be calm. There's a light switch just behind you there. Neil kept the gun extended towards the voice as he fumbled along the wall and flicked the switch.

The light illuminating the room revealed a mid-twenties black man with tight corn-braided hair and a hooded leather jacket. He jerked his head nervously and screwed up his eyes as he observed Neil.

"It's not you...you're not him...but I do know you!"

Neil kept his gun trained on the figure. "Are you Evrol?"

"Yeah...and you're the mystery man from Bournemouth. The one who led us to Stu and Danno that day."

"So you saw me outside the ground then? It was my fault that you found him." Neil raised the gun, levelling it at Evrol's forehead.

"Yeah man, that's right. What are you then...what were you I mean?" He lowered his head slightly.

"Stu was my brother."

"I'm sorry, you must be hurting like we are about Max."

Before Neil could reply, the scrape of a chair leg on the scrubby dance floor caused him to turn and come face to face with a stooped pensioner, wielding a large metal baseball bat.

"Uncle Milton, he's got a gun...put it down! Please put it down." Evrol raised his hands as the old man advanced.

"Think he can walk into my bar threatening family like this?" The old man had receding, greying hair with the texture of a tennis ball, and wore a stained green tracksuit top. Neil flicked the gun between the two men.

"You, get over next to him now!" Neil nodded his head towards Evrol.

"This is my bar you fucking Rasclaat..." The old man continued his advance until Evrol ducked forward and wrenched the bat from his grip and threw it to the floor in front of Neil.

"What you done that for boy?" The old man shoved him and glared angrily at Neil.

"Because he's pointing a gun at us unc'. Calm down man or we'll both end up like Maxie."

"Another fucking stupid white boy. Was always gonna end up in a box." Uncle Milton ignored the gun pointing towards him, and shuffled away behind the bar, leaving Evrol and Neil facing each other down the barrel of the converted starting pistol.

"You know, the old man is probably right about Max. He knew no other way than being a gangster. Me, I've had enough. I want out. If you allow me to walk out of here alive today, I'm going to keep my head down, help my uncle run the club, deal a bit of weed, and spend time with my girlfriend and kids. Leeds is just too fucking dangerous now man. Anyway, how did you find me?"

If Evrol felt his life was at risk, his security arrangements clearly needed some improvement. Neil had started at the obvious place, in Connolly's old boozer. A framed, candle-lit photo of a stocky, dark haired man in his early thirties had held pride of place on the bar of the Waterloo when Neil had entered. A crimson faced barmaid with yellow, tobacco-stained hair had looked up from a quiz book and asked if he was there for Maxie's farewell drink.

Neil had nodded and been told that the rest of the lads were starting in the Fordy and wouldn't be in for a couple of hours. When Neil had confirmed he wanted to chip into the collection to give Max a proper send off, she'd told him Evrol was sorting it.

"He'll be down at' Strega helping his uncle now. Pop down there love, and you'll catch him."

"That easy eh?" Evrol forced a rueful smile. "So now you've found me and I'm looking down the barrel of a gun, what do I need to do to walk out of here alive?"

"Just tell me what you know. What happened between Stuart and Max and why? That's all I want, to understand. I'm not looking for revenge."

Evrol nodded. "I'll tell you what I know man, but it's not a lot. You want a drink? I'd prefer to see a beer in your hand than that." He nodded towards the gun and Neil slowly lowered it and stuck it into the waistband of his jeans.

"Hey old man, two can of Stripe over here for me and my friend."

"Bring it your fucking self!" Uncle Milton continued to crash around behind the counter which was located behind a cage of thick iron bars. Evrol shook his head and stood up, before turning to see Neil reach slowly for the gun.

"It's okay. You can go, I trust you." Neil nodded towards the bar. Shooting Evrol would accomplish nothing. He might be one of the few people who knew what had actually happened to Stuart.

Evrol returned brandishing two ice cold cans of Red Stripe and sat down and lit a fat spliff, which he extended to Neil, who shook his head.

"Just tell me what you know."

"Well, the first thing is obvious. No way did Max top himself like they're saying. I can't say for certain about the two boys, but my guess is the Dutchman did all three of them."

"The Dutchman?"

"Him or the evil looking fucker with the scar and the tattoo."

"Mate, I haven't got a clue what you're on about..." Neil took a swig from the can as Evrol inhaled deeply and blew a thick cloud of weed smoke across the table.

"They turned up the day after Max got out. This Dutch guy who was Connolly's main pills contact and another bloke with a big scar and ink on his neck. Connolly had let too many people have credit on their gear, and they were here to call in the debts. There was also a fair amount of cash missing."

"Like the twenty five grand that Stuart took."

"Yeah that as well. They reckoned Max was the key to collecting what was owed, as he had the local knowledge. Last time I saw him he was heading off to London with this scarfaced foreign guy. He wasn't happy about it, that I do know, as the plan had been for us to do some collecting ourselves." Evrol took a swig of his Red Stripe and knocked the ash from his spliff onto the floor.

"So it was all about collecting what was owed? Nothing to do with Connolly being killed?"

Evrol smiled and shook his head. "Connolly? No man, no one cared about that. Alan Connolly had been a dead man walking for years. He was crazy - a nutter and a total liability. The only surprise was how long it took for someone to do him."

"So he had a few enemies then?" Neil tried to appear disinterested, in case Evrol recalled that he was also on the pier the night Connolly died.

"Too right. He pissed everyone off in those last few months. Totally lost control of the business. Cash and drugs were leaking everywhere. That I know of, he'd had threats from the lads at the Hayfield and the Little Park, some nasty blokes from Bradford and some Chinks in Manchester. That was aside from the stuff with the Dutchman."

"I had wondered if Max blamed Stu and Danno for Connolly and that's why they were killed..."

"You're barking up the wrong tree there my friend, it was nothing to do with Connolly being killed, that I do know." Evrol sat back and scratched at his dreads.

"So what then? Why would this foreign bloke kill Max if he was helping him collect what was owed?" Neil was relieved that he and Julie seemed to be off the hook for Connolly, but it left him no nearer understanding what had happened at his brother's flat.

Evrol shrugged as Uncle Milton shuffled over and slammed two more Red Stripes down on the table.

"Your guess is as good as mine. It makes no sense at all. Maybe the lads got killed because they couldn't pay back the cash, but why they'd do Max too is beyond me."

Uncle Milton growled a low chuckle and stooped low towards the table, encouraging Evrol and Neil to lean in towards him, before addressing them in a hushed tone.

"There's a certain type of man who doesn't need any reason boys. There are some men who can't help themselves. They just love to kill, and once they start, they can't stop."

The old man smiled and shuffled back towards the bar, laughing as he went.

Chapter 16

Wednesday 22 April 1992

Chunnel Delay Likely -The opening of the £9 billion Channel Tunnel may have to be delayed for a second time, it was revealed today. Tunnel operators Eurotunnel announced earlier this year that the opening had been put back to Late Summer 1993. However, major problems which still need to be resolved could now see the long awaited open delayed further.

Knocking the old man to the ground had been a mistake, Le Renard recognised that now. It meant he couldn't go back to the football stadium without risk of arrest. Leeds United had refused to give him Eric's address or phone number, and had now ordered him to stop calling to ask if they'd passed on his message. Kieron at Harlequin's bar had told him that he'd seen a newspaper photo of Eric playing football with his boy in a park near to his home, so it made sense to continue the search there.

An 800 acre tract of parkland, woods and lakes, Roundhay Park was intended to serve as a green lung for the soot-choked inhabitants of Victorian Leeds, four miles to the south. The city boundary had long since extended beyond the park's outer reaches, placing Roundhay within Leeds' northern suburbs, surrounded by an unlikely mix of million pound mansions and apartments, and streets of tired-looking pre-war semis.

Le Renard parked the Renault and climbed out, stretching, and looked at a signboard map of the park which clearly illustrated the needle-in-a-haystack odds that were stacked against him. His entire body ached, and he had cuts and scratches on his hands and arms which he couldn't remember sustaining. His thoughts seemed to be enveloped in a thick fog and his reflexes were sluggish. Another night in Leeds told him what he already knew. This town was no good for him.

Two old ladies sitting on a bench, drinking cups of tea from a flask, watched him take a small, round bundle of cling film from his pocket as he followed the path towards them. They paused their conversation as he approached, and watched him peel open the cling film and dip his index finger into the grey paste, then insert it into his mouth, rubbing it vigorously into his gums as he walked. Le Renard returned their stares as he followed the path uphill, before branching off right along a grassy incline. Reaching the brow of the hill, he looked down into a natural amphitheatre containing a sports pitch and changing rooms. A perfect 180° view of the park extended before him, with paths criss-crossing towards woodland on the left and a playground alongside a lake, visible through the trees to his right. The park was predictably busy on a sunny Wednesday afternoon in the Easter holidays, and Le Renard slowly scanned the figures moving across the landscape before him.

A couple with two dogs. The man was too fat and small to be Eric.

A man running alongside a small child wobbling along on a little cycle. The child looked younger and blonder than the photo he'd seen of Raphael Cantona.

A couple striding up the distant hill. Too old.

A middle aged woman. An elderly man with a child in a pushchair. An Asian family.

"Allez! Où sont vous?" Le Renard muttered as he picked at a pus-filled scab on his knuckle.

Heading down the hill towards the lake he noticed two elderly men on a bench, monitoring his progress. He stared back and fingered the Glock 19 in his jacket.

He passed a wooden café on the lakeside and hurried along a path to a bandstand on the brow of a hill overlooking the distant water. Le Renard sat down and watched a young father spank a screaming toddler, struggling to escape the confines of a push chair. A sudden movement in the distance beyond the buggy caught his attention, and an orange football bounced down the hill, a dark-haired boy of around six in close pursuit. Le Renard glanced across to the left to see the boy's father, wearing a blue tracksuit, strolling towards his son who was now kicking the ball back up the hill. Thick dark hair, gelled into a slight quiff, walking with the straight-backed gait of an athlete. Le Renard felt his heart leap and immediately sprang to his feet.

The man was facing away, jogging to retrieve a wayward pass from the boy, as Le Renard sprinted downhill towards him.

"Eric! C'est moi! C'est Pascal, d'Auxerre." The excited smile on Le Renard's face vanished as the father chipped the ball over his son's head and turned around to face him.

Glasses, a small goatee beard and a confused expression brought the Frenchman's approach to a stuttering halt.

"Fuck. Fucking shit! Merde." Le Renard bent forward, hands on his knees and panting.

"Steady on mate, there's kids around." The father shook his head and moved to the left to trap a full-blooded shot from his boy.

The futility of his situation was now all too apparent to Le Renard. He had no chance of finding Eric in this huge park and he felt the anger rising inside him like a storm. The Glock was out of his pocket and the ghosts urged him on, as he felt the usual calmness begin to descend as he strode forward to end the life of this smug bastard, playing happy families with his son.

The man turned again as he approached, and took a step back as he recognised the intent in the tall stranger's eyes.

"Please mate, I don't want any trouble. I've got my boy here. I only have him one day a week, I'm sorry, I didn't mean owt..."

Le Renard paused and looked around. The couple with the screaming toddler were heading down the slope towards them, and an old woman was making her way up from the lake, tugged along by two greyhounds. If he pulled the trigger, they'd all have to follow, he knew that, as did the ghosts, who laughed and cheered and clapped their blood-soaked hands.

"Okay. It's no problem. I'm sorry. Buy him something." The Frenchman stuffed a red banknote into the pocket of the man's tracksuit top and turned away.

"Wow...thanks mate. You didn't need to..." Le Renard spat and replaced the Glock in his jacket pocket as he walked back up the slope.

He crossed the oval sports field and headed back up the steep slope towards the car park. The two old men were still sitting on a bench beneath a beech tree, and watched him approach.

One of the men shouted something he couldn't hear as he passed around twenty metres in front of the bench, and Le Renard turned and approached them.

"What did you say?" He could now see that the men were in their mid-sixties. Both bore the tanned complexion of the affluent retiree. One was solidly built with a shaved head, wearing three-quarter length shorts and a zipped fleece top. The other, the one who'd shouted, was wiry but muscular for his age, with thinning white hair worn too long at the sides and back, and spiked on top. He wore a purple satin shellsuit, unzipped to mid chest level, revealing a silver pelt of chest hair. Sunglasses with a blue tinted lens obscured his eyes.

"I said it's over there." The elderly man extended his arm over his right shoulder and pointed to an expanse of grass, rolling away towards distant football pitches and a tree-lined road behind him.

Le Renard followed the direction of the man's arm but could see nothing beyond the playing fields, except the distant high-rises of Leeds city centre silhouetted on the horizon beneath a pale blue sky.

"What is over there?"

"Ah, you're foreign. I told you so Gerald.... You lot are usually foreign. Spanish? French?"

Le Renard was in no mood to play games with old men. He sniffed and looked around. No one within earshot. It would take very little to bring the lives of these irritants to a sudden end.

"So where are you from my friend?" The white haired man seemed oblivious to the danger he was in, and removed his shades, rubbing the lenses on his shellsuit top.

"I am from France."

"Yes, of course you are, of course you are. It's over there. Soldier's Field." He jerked a thumb over his shoulder and smirked at the tall figure standing before him.

"I'm sorry, I don't know what you're talking about. What is the soldier's field?"

"Richardson. Claxton. The Ripper...come on, that's what you're looking for isn't it?" The old man looked deep into Le Renard's eyes and for once it was the Frenchman who felt a ripple of discomfort.

"I don't know what this is. I'm sorry..."

"Yorkshire Ripper. Where he killed Richardson. Claxton...the one that got away. He made a mistake there. Very lucky that night was young Peter." The man now stood alongside Le Renard, and he could smell old cigar smoke and aftershave tinged with the chemical aroma of moth balls. The man placed a hand on Le Renard's shoulder and pointed away over the field.

"Over there, under those trees." He spoke softly and slowly, and Le Renard felt himself shiver.

"Go and have a look. Go on, I know you want to." He squeezed Le Renard's shoulder and nudged him with his bony hips.

"Why would I? These things don't interest me." Le Renard took a step away from the old man and fingered the Glock in his jacket pocket. The stockier man sensed the movement, the fear starting to register in his eyes. The white haired man had noticed too, but showed no apprehension. If anything, he seemed amused by the imminent danger and his eyes flashed with excitement.

"I think you are interested though. I know men like you. I know what you are." He glanced down towards the swollen, scabbed knuckles of Le Renard's left hand and smiled a yellow-toothed, rictus grin.

Le Renard clenched his fist and thrust his hand into his pocket, out of sight.

"I am looking for someone, he comes to this park I think."

The white haired man shrugged and joined his friend back on the bench. "Au revoir, mon ami." He waved theatrically and the stocky man smirked.

"Cantona. The footballer. You know him?"

Both the old men ignored the question and stared in silence across the park below them. The brain fog had returned, and Le Renard felt confused and dizzy. In normal circumstances both these old fools would now be lying dead, but he suddenly felt drained of energy, and turned to leave.

"Flying Pizza." He was twenty feet away when he heard the stocky man shout.

"What did you say?"

"Flying Pizza. Five minutes along the road. He's always in there."

Typical Eric. Le Renard smiled as he walked back to the car. Earning big money playing for a top English football team but spends his time in a cheap local Pizza joint.

Ten minutes later, as he squeezed the Renault into a space between a J Reg BMW M3 and a Jaguar XJ220, Le Renard realised he'd clearly underestimated the Flying Pizza. Although it was still the quiet, post-lunch period, the window tables were busy with office groups – women with big hair and shoulder pads, and men in double breasted suits, striped shirts and paisley ties. A head waiter in an electric blue shirt observed Le Renard critically as he peered through the window. His experience told him that no information would be forthcoming concerning the clientele of an establishment like this. Not from the front door anyway.

He ducked down an enclosed alleyway running alongside the restaurant and emerged into another world, one in which he knew would be more useful to him. Back Roman Grove was a narrow street of brick-built semis and scruffy garage units running along the rear of the restaurant. Cigarette butts strewn across the pavement, beside a gate within a high wooden fence told him he was in the right place.

Within fifteen minutes, two men in their late twenties emerged and lit up cigarettes next to the gate. One was overweight, his blue gingham trousers and stained white overall clearly identifying him as kitchen staff. His companion was younger, wearing a lilac shirt and pleated, black trousers and was of Mediterranean appearance. He was disinterested initially when Le Renard told him his story, and explained that alerting the Frenchman the next time Cantona made an appearance at the restaurant was impossible, and was certain to result in his dismissal. Discretion was important to the minor local celebrities who frequented the Flying Pizza.

Two twenty pound notes, and a ten for his friend the chef, were all it needed to change his mind, and persuade him to take Le Renard's number at The Queens.

"He usually comes on a midweek evening, after seven but before nine. He wasn't here yesterday. Maybe he'll come tonight, maybe tomorrow, maybe not at all this week. He never stays too long, you'll have to get here fast."

Le Renard nodded. "I'll be waiting for your call. Please don't let me down, or...just don't let me down please."

Chapter 17

Thursday 23 April 1992

Bonded! United Fans Splash out £2m – Leeds United's £500 'money back' bond scheme has raised close to £2m towards the cost of the new £5m all-seater East Stand, it was revealed today. Work on the new stand, on the site of the current Lowfields Road stand is due to start at the end of the current season.

"What are these then?" the young man in the passenger seat looked suspiciously at DI Andy Barton's outstretched hand, which held a sheath of red and white paper.

"Fucking rocking horse shit is what they are. Here, take them..." Barton thrust the tickets towards him and the young man held one up to the light.

"They look real."

"They are real 'Mr. Hunter'. Fifteen tickets for Sunday's game. A gift."

"Shoreham Road End. That's their Kop. You're giving me fifteen tickets for Sheff United's end?"

"Blocks of five, in three consecutive rows, four back from the front. A rectangle, just to the left of the goal. Perfect formation." Andy Barton scratched at his moustache and looked out into the gloom of the Merrion Centre multi storey.

"Perfect formation? What the fuck are you on about?" The young man flicked through the tickets, shaking his head.

"Fifteen handy lads in three rows together will have no bother. Make yourselves known when Leeds score, or just before full time if it's still nil-nil then. There'll just be kids, grannies and disabled in front of you, so you'll only have to fight a rearguard action, there's no fence, so it's straight over onto the cinder track. Try and make sure you do it while the ball is down that end though, so the cameras definitely pick it up." Andy Barton turned to face the young man who was staring back at him, open mouthed.

"You're actually serious, aren't you?"

Andy Barton puffed out his cheeks and exhaled loudly.

"No other choice now."

"What do you mean no other choice? Choice about what?" The young man turned to face Barton.

"Well, those names you provided gave us absolutely nothing. A few press cuttings and some odds and ends that could be classed as weapons in the houses, but nothing we could take to trial..."

"For fuck's sake! That's what I told you all along, you fucking idiot. What did you expect, a detailed dossier on hooligan operations with' names of all' lads involved?"

"That's more or less what we got in Wild Boar."

"Jesus Christ." The young man cradled his head in his hands and sat back, looking at the roof of the Cavalier. Andy Barton continued to stare ahead through the windscreen.

"So, we need a new approach. Something big. Attention grabbing. Scrapping in the stands and a pitch invasion live on telly at the title decider should get a decent amount of press coverage..."

"And you just expect me to turn up with fifteen lads, kick off in full view of hundreds of South Yorkshire law and the television cameras, get nicked and probably battered, just to get you out of a hole? You're fucking deranged man..."

"You won't get charged. It won't go to court anyway. And fifteen of your best lads can handle the BBC can't you?" Barton spoke quietly. He'd thought this one through and the plan was sound, if he could just get the Leeds firm to execute it.

"What do you mean it won't go to court, how do you know?"

"Where do you think the tickets came from?"

"Bramall Lane I'm guessing. Are you trying to tell me they're okay with this, a bit of added excitement for the family section?"

Barton paused, as if considering whether to confide in the young man, then turned towards him, a smug half smile on his lips.

"The tickets came from Sheffield's FIO. He's on board with this."

"Sheffield's spotter? Their police want us in their end?"

Barton nodded. "He has a different problem to me. Has a few faces he needs to catch in the act, as it were, so you lot can be the bait."

"That's nice..." The young man shook his head and lit a cigarette.

"My problem is a little more...complex. And political. Ironically, to solve my problem, we need to actually create a problem. Correction, you need to create a problem..."

"So what you're saying is you want us to kick off in' ground on live TV, get' game stopped for a bit so it makes' press and we all get nicked. Then it all gets brushed under' carpet, but you get on Look North and Calendar again to talk about the resurgence of football violence."

"Clever lad. I think you've just about got the measure of it."

The young man sucked hard on his cigarette and wound down the window to exhale a cloud of smoke. Andy Barton turned on the ignition. Job done.

"The thing that confuses me..." The young man flicked his cigarette through the open window.

"Yeah?"

"Is why the fucking hell you think I'd go along with this pile of shit?"

Andy Barton turned off the ignition.

"Because we all win, that's why." He spoke slowly, remaining calm. The plan was perfect, and he'd assumed the incentive of fifteen tickets for the match would seal the deal, but the face of the young man in his passenger seat told Barton that he was far from convinced.

"How's that then?"

"Well, as I explained, it solves the problem I have with my big bosses. It re-establishes the hooligan threat as a problem in the media. That puts them under pressure. Bumps it up their list of priorities if you like..."

"Doesn't help me. Go on..."

"It provides you with fifteen highly desirable match tickets."

"We're sorted for tickets."

"Real ones?"

"Mostly. We'll get in. Don't worry about us." The young man lit his last cigarette and tossed the packet out of the window.

"It also solves the issue of our arrangement. You've given me nothing and I still have the evidence to send you down remember?"

The cigarette glowed orange and the young man scowled and narrowed his eyes.

"That's right. You still have a debt to pay. Plus, it gives you a free hit at the BBC, live on telly. Imagine the respect for the lads who give it to them in their own end at the last away game of the season..." Barton grinned, confident that he'd now ticked all the right boxes.

"You really don't get it do you?" The lad was smiling as well now, turning towards him, blowing smoke into Andy Barton's face. "Call yourself football intelligence but you haven't got a fucking clue, have you?"

"What? About what?"

"It's the fucking league title decider for fuck's sake. Probably the biggest game me and my mates have ever been to, maybe ever will. The only chance we've had to see Leeds actually win summat after years of watching total shite. Who do you think is going to give us any respect for kicking off in' ground and missing our biggest game for twenty years?"

Barton looked ahead, drumming on the steering wheel.

"Go on...who do you think is going to congratulate us, say well done lads, what a fucking great idea that was? Eh? Go on...?

"Rest of' lads will, I'm sure." Andy Barton chewed his lip, eyes stinging from second-hand cig smoke.

"Rest of what lads?...go on say it?"

"Say what?"

"Rest of' Service Crew. That's what you wanted to say wasn't it? For fuck's sake." The young man laughed so hard it turned into a cough, which culminated in him expelling a gob of phlegm from the car window.

"How many times do I have to tell you? It's over, has been for nearly ten years. There is no Service Crew, no organised firm. You're too late. You're trying to relive the eighties, make it like it was before you lot fucked it up with your CCTV and banning orders. Lads don't want to risk getting locked up now, they want to watch the game then go out after, drop a pill and dance. Peace and love and all that shit. And this game more than any...there's no way I'm missing this one." The young man nudged the car door open with his knee and got out and began walking away.

"Alright, you don't need to be in their end. Just get the tickets to the right lads...please." Barton was out of the car, hands resting on the roof.

The young man paused and looked back over his shoulder.

"And that clears my debt? The evidence disappears?"

"Yes, I'll make sure of that. Just make sure it goes off and the lads get on the pitch, stop the game for a few minutes. Trust me, do this and I'll wipe the slate clean. All forgotten."

The young man nodded and zipped his jacket up tight under his chin and began to walk away, before pausing and turning to face Barton.

"I'll see what I can do. And you can stop with all this fucking Hunter bollocks then too."

Chapter 18

Le Renard had woken late again, feeling listless, struggling to focus and with more unremembered bruises and lesions on his hands and arms. He'd called a number written on a scrap of paper, and half an hour later, a battered F Reg Orion had pulled up outside the front door of the Queens. The hook-nosed driver was clearly a peasant from the Northern Tribal regions of Pakistan – some off-grid, mud-hut hamlet in the badlands of Khyber or Mohmand or North Waziristan. An illiterate farmhand brought to the West by a dowry arrangement to marry his first cousin. These people were only good for guns and heroin, and it was the latter which Le Renard craved.

He'd sniffed with displeasure as he'd climbed into the back seat of the filthy mini cab. The smell had turned his stomach and he'd wound down the window and coughed. It seemed that the driver spoke little English, but he'd clearly known where to go, and quickly delivered his passenger to a red brick terraced house near the football stadium. Here Le Renard had paid over the odds for some cheap, badly cut heroin and shot it up in a filthy kitchen, watched by a shit-stained toddler and its semi-comatose mother.

"You're a fucking disgrace. Clean yourself up."

He'd tossed the teenage girl a red bank note, and she'd stared vacantly at the tall stranger injecting himself over her sink of filthy crockery, and cackled at the irony. He'd turned away, sickened by the sight of a scabbed mouth filled with brown stumps.

Then it was back to the hotel, feeling calmer, more able to focus. A shower and a line of his employer's finest produce and he'd been ready to go to work.

He'd had a bad feeling about the final collection for the Dutchman, at a garage unit in an industrial estate to the east of the city centre. On his first visit the previous week, the overweight, shaven headed owner had lied unconvincingly about the ten Ceska Zbrojovka CZ82's that he still hadn't paid Connolly for. Over a chipped mug of sweet tea and a packet of biscuits, Le Renard had allowed him to talk for several minutes about how he'd been unable to move the guns on, and had eventually passed them back to Connolly. The Frenchman had then placed his cup on the makeshift table created from three upturned tyres, smiled and leant slowly towards the fat man, as if about to share an intriguing secret. The man had fallen silent and tilted his head sidewards, before letting out an animal cry of terror as Le Renard had bitten off his lower ear then spat it into one of the steaming mugs of tea.

Unsurprisingly, the garage owner had then agreed to retrieve the weapons within the week, but as he'd driven away, Le Renard had detected something more than raw fear in the eyes of the blood-soaked man watching him from the workshop doorway. Something closer to pure hatred and a desire for revenge.

He'd therefore arrived half an hour earlier than the arranged 3pm meeting, and parked the Renault a quarter of a mile down the road. A route through the fence of a disused factory and over a small stone wall had brought him to the rear door of the garage unit. The fat man had still been directing his two accomplices as Le Renard had crept in, silent and unannounced, and watched as they acted out the planned scenario which was to occur as the Frenchman entered through the main sliding doors. How the tall, thin Asian teenager would bring the lump hammer down upon his head, and how the heavyset youth with lank, centre parted hair would then administer the coup-de-grace with a large kitchen knife.

They'd still been rehearsing, planning the finer details, straightening the edges of the plastic tarpaulin into which his body would fall, when Le Renard had stepped forward from the shadows, raised the Glock and blown away the side of the Asian's face. The fat man and the lank haired youth had been frozen to the spot, mouths agape, as they'd watched their friend fall against the sliding door. Then the youth had pissed himself, just before Le Renard had put a neat hole in the centre of his forehead. The fat man had begun to say something, staggering forward, arms aloft and eyes wide with terror. In years gone by, the Frenchman could have entertained himself for the whole afternoon, by very slowly ending the life of the overweight fool with the shaven head and the poorly drawn tattooed arms. Now though, he'd lost interest. A single shot through the mouth had blown a six inch exit wound in the back of the man's head. Le Renard had removed a biro from his pocket and placed a thick ink cross on his list, then he'd headed back to the hotel.

He'd needed an hour-long soak in a hot bath with a half pint glass of brandy and a gram bag of cocaine to rid himself of the stench of blood and filth from the garage job, and was lying on the bed, half-heartedly masturbating to Blockbusters on the TV when the phone on the bedside table rang.

"He's here, with his wife and another couple. My shift just started and he was already here when I arrived so you'll need to be quick."

"Okay, thank you."

Twenty minutes later, Le Renard pulled up and parked on the road opposite the restaurant. No space in front of the windows, beneath the red awning with its white lettering spelling out 'Flying Pizza'. No space unless you slipped the concierge a banknote as you left, and asked him to save you one out front next time, as the owners of the H Reg Range Rover, the J Reg Merc and personal number plate Porsche Carrera had clearly done.

Le Renard tilted the rear-view mirror and grimaced at his reflection. The sunken, grey, sallow skin of his cheeks accentuated the thick, black rings beneath his eyes. A slight cut within a raised lump on his forehead hinted at a recent, unrecalled headbutt, and a weeping herpetic sore in the corner of his mouth bled a yellow discharge onto his chin. This city with its cheap sex, dirty drugs and drunken, hard-faced citizens had been no good for him, that was for sure. He tilted his head towards the light and ran his finger along the length of the scar which separated his face into diagonal halves. He'd changed in ten years. He was a different person to the young man who worked at the bar in Auxerre. It was no surprise that Eric hadn't remembered him.

He then caught sight of the cruel eyes of the fox on his neck, its mouth curled into a sneer, reminding him, as it did every day, of who he was. What he was, what he'd become since Auxerre. He wanted to take the knife from his jeans pocket and plunge it deep into that smirking vulpine face, hack away at his own flesh until it was gone, until he felt clean again. The ghosts in his head whispered their encouragement. There was no need now though. The ritual cleansing of his sins would begin when Eric listened to his story. Redemption felt close.

Le Renard monitored the comings and goings through the restaurant's glass doors. Balding, middle aged Jews in suit jackets and open necked shirts, what remained of their hair brushed back and worn long over the collar. Their women, orange make-up and big earrings, shoulder pads and knee-length skirts worn too tight around their skinny arses. Le Renard cleared his nostrils and spat through the car window. His distaste for this overlit suburban Pizza joint, with its try-too-hard clientele was growing by the minute.

Then, amidst the frequent opening and closing of the door, Le Renard watched the head waiter in his bright blue shirt paying too much attention to a middle-aged man with a bald head, who was holding the door open for others behind him. Wearing a suit jacket and open necked shirt and glasses with thick red frames, the man was shaking hands with the head waiter, smiling, laughing. He stepped through the door, followed by a woman with blonde, shoulder length hair, wearing red heels, jeans and a short denim jacket. Behind her came a shorter woman, wearing a shapeless, blue top and black leggings. Dark hair worn in a high pony-tail, with a thick fringe falling over an elfin face and full lips highlighted red. He recognised her from the newspaper clippings he'd collected over the years. Isabelle.

Le Renard's heart leapt, and he was already sprinting across Street Lane when Eric emerged from the restaurant. Smiling shyly, embarrassed by the attention from the overbearing restaurant employee, dressed in a simple lilac sweatshirt, baggy denim jeans and white trainers, Le Renard felt that he'd stepped back in time, to the day he first saw Eric at the bar in Auxerre.

The bald man flicked at a key fob and the lights of a black BMW parked in front of the restaurant blinked in recognition. The two women climbed into the back seat and the bald man with the red glasses opened the driver's door, as Le Renard raced to intercept Eric as he moved towards the passenger side. His heart pounded in his chest. His moment of redemption was here.

"Eric! C'est Pascal, de le bar Chatte Noir d'Auxerre. Je dois vous parlez!" He called out as Eric opened the car door and clambered in alongside the driver.

"Bonsoir." Eric smiled at Le Renard and closed the car door as the tall stranger stooped to peer in at him.

"C'est moi Eric, Pascal, d'Auxerre. Vous souvient pas de moi?"

Le Renard's manic grin split the herpes sore, and he loomed over the car, blood and pus smeared on his chin, tears in his eyes, urging Eric to remember, to listen to his story. Cantona turned and said something to the man sat beside him, as the BMW engine burst into life and the reversing lights flashed white.

"Pourquoi est-ce que je t'aime Eric? Pourquoi? Je ne sais pas pourquoi, mais je t'aime!" Le Renard raised his voice, stooping to look into the car, but Eric was still speaking to the driver and didn't see the tall, thin man with the tear-stained face and heaving chest who peered at him through the passenger side window.

The head waiter in the blue shirt had been monitoring the situation through the glass door and now stepped outside, holding a cordless phone, as the BMW slowly reversed out towards Street Lane.

"Hey, please stop a' bothering my customers. Or do I need to call a' police?"

"No. I am Eric's biggest fan. I am not here to hurt him. I have something important to tell him." Le Renard breathed heavily and sobbed and looked down at the soiled Queens Hotel slippers on his feet.

"Well, I think this is no possible. Eric has a big game coming up at the weekend. Hey, you like'a football?" The waiter was smiling and attempted to lighten the mood in his heavily accented English.

"Fucking go away or I will open up your throat." Le Renard hissed as he watched the black BMW pause, waiting for a gap in the early evening traffic heading towards Roundhay Park.

"Okay, that's it. I call a' police." The waiter hurried back through the doors, tapping on the cordless phone as Le Renard blinked through his tears, watching as a Mondeo flashed its lights, allowing the BMW to reverse out onto the road.

Le Renard sank to his knees and the tyres of the BMW screeched as it arced in a U-Turn across Street Lane. From the driver's seat, the bald man cast a glance towards the tall stranger kneeling on the pavement, with the tear stained, scarred face, the fox head tattoo and the Queen's Hotel slippers, pointing at the car and spitting out inaudible words.

Le Renard watched the BMW accelerate away along the tree lined avenue, then sank forward, his forehead pressed hard into the tarmac, and sobbed like a child.

When he looked up, he saw that he was being watched from the window by the middle-aged Jews in their suit jackets and open necked shirts, and their orange faced, skinny arsed women, and the driver of the Range Rover and the Mercedes and the Porsche, all laughing, enjoying the free show.

Then the head waiter in the bright blue shirt with the cordless phone appeared in the doorway of the restaurant and started shouting in his fucking Italian pidgin English, telling him that the police were on their way, and he was going to jail, and in that moment, Le Renard decided. There was only one way he knew to calm the percussive thumping in his ribcage and quieten the mocking laughter of the ghosts. He would kill them all. The waiter in the blue shirt, the Jews, the orange faced women, the Porsche and Mercedes drivers and all the rest of them.

He stood up slowly and looked towards the restaurant and the head waiter stopped talking into the phone. Le Renard's right hand moved instinctively towards his left underarm, feeling for his jacket pocket and the Glock. The jacket which was hanging from the back of a chair in his room at The Queens, left behind, along with his shoes in the rush to get to Eric.

Through his tears, Le Renard began to laugh and shouted towards the restaurant.

"I think you have a guardian angel watching over you today. Eric once had his angel too, but who will save him now? Who?"

The waiter locked the glass doors as the tall, tattooed man with the tear stained, scarred face and the Queens Hotel slippers staggered forward, now laughing manically.

"Who will save him now? His angel has become a devil. Who will save us both?"

Now he knew it was over. There would be no redemption. They were both on the wrong path and he was the only one who could put it right. He turned quickly and walked across Street Lane without looking, not hearing the car horns or the screech of tyres, only the mocking taunts of the ghosts in his head.

'Il ne vous ecouterez pas! Il ne vous connaît même pas!' He won't listen to you...he doesn't even know you!'

The ghosts cheered and laughed and clapped their blood-soaked hands, and Le Renard knew there was only one way to silence them for good. Only one way to end his eternal suffering now.

Chapter 19

Friday 24 April 1992

Now its 3-1 on for United – Leeds United, on the brink of their first League Championship for 18 years are the new 3-1 on title favourites. Manchester United's 1-0 defeat at bottom of the table West Ham last night leaves Leeds in charge of their own destiny in the crucial last ten days of the season. Manchester Utd manager Alex Ferguson virtually conceded the championship, saying 'Leeds are in the driving seat now. It's as simple as that.'

"Good morning Sergeant Barton, come in, take a seat." Phillip Holloway didn't look up from the papers he was scribbling on, as Andy Barton pushed open the office door.

"It's Inspector, sir." Barton tugged a leather chair from beneath the desk and sat down opposite his boss.

"Hmmm, yes. Anyway, a couple of things. First, it's the last away game of the season on Sunday. Local derby too obviously, and an absolutely critical game for Leeds United. Could potentially decide the league championship from what I've been reading?"

"That's correct sir. Man Utd have lost two matches in a row, and Leeds are a point ahead now, and Manchester have to play away at Liverpool on Saturday. If Leeds win and Man.U lose, Leeds win the league." Barton smiled. He preferred Rugby League, but after witnessing the team's struggles over the last decade, it would be good to see some success. A boost for the city and the genuine supporters. Phillip Holloway looked back impassively.

"Righto. If that weren't to happen though, I'm guessing there would be a risk of serious disorder at the Sheffield stadium. Most likely a full scale riot, worse than the scenes we saw there back in '85?"

"Well, there is also a home game left against Norwich sir, so I'm not sure the fans would react that badly on Sunday. It is a midday kick off too, which does reduce..."

Phillip Holloway stood up and sighed loudly to cut him off in mid sentence. He walked to the window and opened the blinds, allowing a shaft of sunlight to momentarily blind Barton.

"This Norwich game then. If Leeds were to fall at that final hurdle and lose the title to Manchester, I'm guessing the fans would be ruddy angry?" Holloway turned back to face Barton who had tilted his head to the left to avoid the sun's beam.

"Well obviously sir, but I think the general feeling would be that the team have exceeded..."

"Do they have a 'firm'?"

"I'm sorry sir...do who have a firm?" Barton was struggling to keep up.

"Norwich. Is there a big rivalry there? Serious disorder likely?"

"Erm no...not really. Sir, look I think I know where you're going with this..."

"Oh really? And where is that then? And before you reply Sergeant, let me be very clear that my over-riding concern here is the protection of the public via the prevention of any serious disorder in or around football stadia. Go ahead."

Barton paused and selected his words carefully.

"Sir, our intelligence suggests that serious, large scale disorder at either of the remaining fixtures is unlikely..." Barton spotted Holloway's eyes roll and heard the sigh which generally indicated that he'd been given the wrong answer.

"However, sir, our sources inform us that members of an organised hooligan group have managed to obtain tickets for the Sheffield section of the stadium."

Holloway's eyes lit up.

"The Service Crew?"

"We believe so sir, yes. We also understand they've made contact with counterparts in Sheffield's main risk group."

"Their name again?"

"They call themselves the Blades Business Crew sir."

"Hmmm, both 'crews'. Disappointing..." Holloway was waving his fountain pen like an imaginary Stanley knife.

"Sir?"

"'Firm' sounds much better in the media. More sinister and organised. I think when you talk to the press after the game you should refer to the Blades Business Firm, yes?"

"Well, yes sir, of course. I must emphasise that although this is reliable intelligence, we can't be 100% certain that disorder will occur."

Phillip Holloway nodded, closed the blinds and sat down opposite Barton.

"I understand, but if it does, our intelligence will allow us to identify the perpetrators quickly, that is, dawn raids to be executed during the following week with the media in attendance?"

"I believe so, yes sir."

" Very good Andy. Now the other matter I mentioned." Holloway lowered his voice and leant across the desk.

"We have something of a ...situation, which you may be aware of, if you've spoken to any of the CID boys in the canteen?"

"These gangland murders? Some sort of hitman on the loose, torturing and killing local criminals? I have heard a few whispers on the grapevine."

"Mmmm. Nasty old business, though he's actually done us a few favours, hence the light-touch approach we've taken up to now." Holloway smirked and nodded, which Barton took as the green light to issue a forced laugh.

"The thing is, this particular problem may now have extended into your remit somewhat."

"My remit sir? Football intelligence?"

"Unfortunately so Andy. It seems a chap going by a similar description to that of the suspect, scarred face, prominent tattoo, caused a bit of a scene at Elland Road last week. Then some character with a similar description kicked up a fuss at a restaurant some French player had been dining at."

Barton paused and blinked, shaking his head slightly.

"Cantona? Erm, I'm not sure sir how..."

"Yes Andy, I agree that this isn't your normal bread and butter, but the club are concerned that this chap may attempt something at Sunday's match. He's clearly unbalanced, so I need you and your team to be aware and keep an eye out. And make sure South Yorkshire are alerted too. Officers on the turnstiles provided with his description, that type of approach. And there's another thing..."

Barton sighed and nodded.

"Our intelligence suggests that the same suspect may be involved in the deaths of the three Leeds men in London. The brother of one of the Service Crew generals was one of those killed I believe?"

"Well, erm, yes sir. The older Yardsley brother is a member of the main risk group."

"Very good. So, this sits firmly within your remit I'd say."

Holloway stood and walked towards the door which he opened as Andy Barton vacated his seat.

" Oh and Sergeant..."

Barton turned and was about to correct Holloway on his rank again until he saw his face.

"Please don't let the side down on Sunday. It's a big day as you know, and we need to ensure we get the right sort of headlines. I'm sure you understand what I mean."

Andy Barton hadn't time to respond before his boss closed the door in his face.

Chapter 20

Sunday 26 April 1992

"What the fuck is this about? I'm going to miss' kick off now." The young man in the mustard-coloured Stone Island anorak was arguing with two uniformed constables, who'd apprehended him as he stepped through the Bramall Lane turnstiles, and now guided him to the far end of the draughty, concrete concourse which was echoing to the distant strains of Marching on Together from the terraces above.

"Good morning 'Mr Hunter'." Andy Barton stepped from behind a pillar, wearing a padded anorak and blue baseball cap.

"Oh for fuck's sake what do you want now?" The young man stopped and thrust his hands deep into his jacket pockets.

"Thanks officers, you can go now, I'll handle this." Barton indicated with a flick of the head that this was to be a private meeting.

"What's with all' coppers on' turnstiles checking everyone? Took ages to get in." The young man glanced at his watch and nervously shifted his weight from foot to foot.

"Some nutter harassing Cantona."

"Fucking hell, what, like a stalker?"

Barton looked over his shoulder and lowered his voice.

"Apparently some sort of gangland hitman, if word on the street is correct...and I shouldn't tell you this, but as we're...partners as it were..."

"Fuck off," the young man laughed under his breath.

"...It may be of interest to know that they think he was the one who topped Yardsley's brother in London."

That got the young man's attention.

"He killed Neil's kid? Fucking hell, does Yards know?"

"No one knows, so keep it to yourself. CID are meant to be all over it, but the useless twats can't track him down, even though he's meant to have a scar like Zorro right across his face and a fox's head tattooed on his neck." Barton shook his head and snorted a laugh. "Total useless cunts."

"Anyway, how did you lot get down here? Not on the train. In fact, there were hardly any lads on the train. Managed to get on a bus have you?" Barton leant across and straightened the compass emblem on the young man's arm.

"Get off that...We came in cars and one of' lads van. No time for walking back to town and fucking about with trains today. Everyone wants to be back to watch' Scum game. Anyway, I wasn't aware I had to get you to approve our travel plans..."

Barton smirked. "I don't care how you get here, but I do care what happens once you're here. I've seen Yardsley, Hurst and the rest come in here with you, which means they aren't in the Sheffield Kop."

"I can see why you're a copper. How long did that take to work out?"

"Very funny...so who's got my fucking tickets?"

"Leeds fans." The young man turned and waved in response to a shout from a lad further down the concourse.

"Leeds fans or Leeds hooligans?" Barton moved closer, no longer smiling.

"Is there a difference? How the fuck do I know?"

"I gave you those tickets on the understanding they were going to proper lads, not fucking shirt-wearing supporters club types." The young man stood his ground as Barton jabbed a finger into his chest.

"What's up with' supporters clubs? You get some good lads on' supporters club buses. Look at 'Pioneer, Kippax, Gildersome..."

"You'll be telling me next you gave them to the fucking University branch. So, you're confident that our plan is going to come off in the next 90 minutes?" Barton lowered his voice and stepped back as late arriving supporters dashed past, with a roar from above indicating that the game had begun.

"Our plan..? Where did OUR plan come from? This is YOUR fucking plan mate, nothing to do with me..." The young man turned and began walking away.

"Big 90 minutes coming up 'Mr Hunter.' Something big better happen behind that goal or I'll be looking for another job and you'll be watching your arse in the showers in Armley."

The young man turned and winked.

"The game's started. Come on or you'll miss all the action."

Chapter 21

"That goal was mental. It was like pinball in their box.And couldn't be a better time to equalise, 47th minute!"

Neil and Hursty were queuing for coffee and pies in the cavernous concourse of Sheffield United's away end. A scrappy first half, spoilt for football purists by a swirling wind, had at least served up plenty of incident, with the Blades' early lead being cancelled out by Rod Wallace's ricocheted equaliser.

"We'll go on to win this now, I can feel it." Hursty turned to his best mate. "Would be a right tribute wouldn't it mate, to win it this year for Stu and Danno?"

Neil smiled momentarily before catching the eye of Andy Barton, pushing through the crowd towards them.

"Looks like he's on a mission." Neil nodded and the lads watched Barton push his way into the gent's toilet.

Barton walked along the lines of men facing the piss-stained urinals until he located his target, then yanked him backwards by the hood of his jacket, shoving him into an empty toilet cubicle.

"What the fuck just happened?"

"Jesus I've pissed on my trainers, what's up with you?"

Barton was nose to nose with the young man, spittal frothing in the corner of his mouth, eyes flashing with anger.

"What's up with me? We had a fucking arrangement! Fifteen tickets. I made promises to Sheffield's FIO. Told him our boys knew the score and it would go off when Leeds scored. What happened?"

"Kicked off a bit. I saw a couple of lads windmilling a bit and a few got taken out."

"Kicked off a bit? I didn't see a single punch thrown, let alone a pitch invasion, and the cameras were facing down the other end. What a disaster, a total fucking disaster!" Barton now held the young man by the throat and he struggled to stay upright, his legs straddling either side of the pebble-dashed toilet bowl.

"Woah, lads calm it down, we're about to win the title!" A fat, balding man in a blue Leeds anorak was sent into retreat as Barton turned towards him.

"I'm a police officer. Fuck off if you don't want to get nicked." The man raised his hands and reversed from the cubicle, as Barton turned back to face the now purple-faced youth. "You don't know what you've done, you fucking idiot. You've ruined everything, it's going to have to be Norwich now. Something massive as well..."

"Norwich? Are you serious? You've fucking lost it Barton." The young man wrenched the hand from his throat and shoved Barton back outside the cubicle, causing supporters at the urinals to turn and stare.

"Why don't you tell everyone in here why you're so pissed off, Sergeant or Inspector or whatever the fuck it was they made you? Tell everyone the plan?"

Barton inhaled deeply and looked down at the piss soaked concrete floor of the toilets.

"No I thought not. If that's all you've got, I'm off back to watch' second half." The young man backed away then turned and headed towards the door.

"You're fucking finished Sutcliffe, you mark my words."

The young man turned and smiled.

"Sutcliffe now is it? What happened to Hunter then?"

"Hunter's dead. The same as you will be when all your mates find out that you've been grassing them up for the last year." Barton inhaled through his nose to summon a mouthful of phlegm which he expelled loudly onto the toilet floor.

"Goodbye Mr Sutcliffe, I think your time is up."

Chapter 22

"Jesus...Could go either way this game." Neil hauled Hursty back up the packed terrace following another surge forward, as Gary Speed's shot ricocheted off the Blades post, and Mcallister's volleyed rebound sailed high over the bar.

"Yeah, the wind's playing havoc. I'm not sure if it's helping them or us more."

A few minutes later, they almost had an answer as a long ball booted downfield from the Sheff United keeper was picked up by the wind, and found Brian Deane who unleashed a half volley that Lukic just managed to tip over the Leeds bar.

The extreme nervous energy in the Leeds end, coupled with the strange, split-tiered layout of the away stand led to a muted, almost surreal atmosphere – The Leeds fans in the lower terracing couldn't hear those in the seats above them and vice versa, and the tense atmosphere seemed to be cascading down from the stand onto the pitch, with both teams making repeated errors.

"Bollocks, he's clear again." Hursty covered his eyes as Deane closed in on the Leeds goal with only Lukic to beat, but the keeper managed to push his shot wide.

"Too close for comfort that lads eh?" Neil turned to see Young Sutcliffe push through the crowd and take up position on the step behind him.

"Yeah, we definitely need a goal to settle the nerves."

"Free kick ref, fucking hell!"

Neil grimaced as Hursty reacted to a foul on Batty by yelling inches from his ear.

"Come on Macca, swing it in."

It seemed as though the Leeds number ten had heard the instruction, as a perfectly weighted cross evaded Rees in the Sheffield goal, to be met by the stooping figure of Jon Newsome on the far post, who sent the ball spinning into the Blades' goal.

It took a couple of seconds for the Leeds fans at the opposite end of the stadium to register the rippling of the net and embark on a frenzied celebration. Hursty disappeared down the terrace and into the crowd, and Neil found himself locked in an embrace with Young Sutcliffe.

Neil looked at his watch."65 minutes gone. This is going to be a long half hour."

Sutcliffe remained silent as the whole stand began to shake, with the upper and lower tiers finally coming together as a single bouncing, deafening entity.

"E-I E-I E-I O, up the football league we go,

when we win the title, this is what we'll sing,

We are the champions, we are the champions, Sergeant Wilko's team!"

Hursty still hadn't reappeared, and Neil and Sutcliffe had barely caught their breath after the goal, when a loose ball ricocheted off Speed for a Sheffield corner. Gannon swung the ball into the Leeds box, and again the swirling wind caused panic as it evaded everyone, before falling to Pemberton on the edge of the six yard box. His hopeful stab back towards goal caught the shin of Lee Chapman and the ball bounced into the Leeds goal. Their lead had lasted all of three minutes.

"Ah shite. That was bound to happen."

Neil turned round, expecting to be met by a face full of angry rage, but Sutcliffe just nodded and gave a rueful smile, seeming almost detached from the action.

Leeds continued to pile forward seeking a priceless winning goal, and the agitation in the crowd was palpable. Neil muttered instructions under his breath and urged the team on, with Sutcliffe remaining impassive behind him. A long distance drive from Batty rebounded away for a corner and a crowd surge propelled Neil forward. Sutcliffe hauled him back into place.

"Wasn't sure you'd be here today mate, what with your brother and all that. Sorry to hear about that..."

Stuart's death had been something of an elephant in the room on the forty mile journey down the M1. Beyond some muttered 'sorry about your kid ' comments, only Hursty had asked how Neil was feeling, until now, and Young Sutcliffe was an unexpected source of sympathy.

"Yeah, it's been a tough week but there's not much I can do. They haven't released his body yet, so I thought I might as well be here as sat at home. He'd have wanted me to come too, he'd definitely have been here himself."

Sutcliffe nodded and fell silent again before leaning in towards Neil again.

"You've been coming a long time...do you remember' last league title?"

"74? Yeah a bit. I was nine. My dad took me to' last home game against Ipswich. I don't remember much about it though." Neil tilted his head backwards and shouted over his shoulder.

"I was only four then. My first game was Wolves just before Christmas 1979. We won 3-0. Connor, Graham and Gary Hamson scored. I was nine, It was a Christmas present off my dad. Not a great one when you think about it, we've always been shit while I've watched us." Sutcliffe spoke quietly, almost as if he was talking to himself, and Neil was struggling to hear him.

"Yeah, it was the same for Stu. At least I got to see the end of the Revie team, even though I was too young to really appreciate it. Just thought it would always be like that....Mcallister's going off. Who's this coming on?"

"Think it's Cantona. Looks like we're going for it then..."

"Yep...I'd be happy with a point actually." Neil applauded as the Leeds number ten jogged across the pitch.

"It will be a big thing, won't it?"

"What will?" Neil turned again, and pushed backwards up the step to create a space to stand alongside Sutcliffe.

"Winning the league. Would be a massive thing really, after all' shit years. Shit players, shit away grounds, shit managers. I was even too young to go away in the mid eighties when at least you lot had a laugh every week."

"Yeah, winning it the second year after promotion would be unbelievable. Going up was big, but this would be the next level. European Cup again, Milan, Barcelona, Madrid, that's hard to believe when you think of the places we were going a few years back." Sutcliffe didn't respond and Neil glanced towards him in time to see him dab at his eye with a coat sleeve.

"Grit in my eye. This wind is blowing a load of shit around. Go on Batts, get stuck in..."

Neil turned back towards the pitch, where the bright spring sun lit up a swirling tornado of wind-blown crisp packets and burger wrappers in front of a Sheffield throw-in.

"You've never really liked me have you?"

"What?" Neil didn't turn to face Sutcliffe. They were stood shoulder to shoulder and the conversation was starting to feel too awkward.

"Ever since you came out of' nick. We've never really got on..."

Neil shrugged. "I only see you two or three times a month mate, I don't really know you.... well played Newsome...he's done alright against Deane today." Neil was eager to turn the conversation back to the match.

"Nah, I could always tell. You thought I was a wanker."

"You're a few years younger than me. I'd done all that stuff you wanted to do, seen it wasn't worth it, so I just thought you were naïve that's all. A bit daft..." Neil smiled, hoping to lighten the mood.

"I think you were right." Sutcliffe muttered under his breath and Neil struggled to catch his reply.

"What's brought all this on anyway?"

"Nowt. It's just...I know summat..." Sutcliffe's words were lost in the noise of the crowd as a Sheffield free kick was hoisted towards the Leeds penalty area, hanging in the wind before being hacked clear by Speed.

"Go on Cantona...sorry mate, what did you say?" The ball bobbled in the centre circle and, under pressure from Rod Wallace, a Sheffield defender sent it looping back high into the swirling wind.

"I don't know if I should tell you..." Sutcliffe leant in towards Neil and raised his voice, as Blades' centre half Brian Gayle tried to shepherd the bouncing ball into his own penalty area, under pressure from the advancing Wallace and Cantona.

"Tell me what?...go on Eric!" Gayle, now facing his own goal and onrushing keeper, panicked and knocked the ball skyward with his knee.

"It's about your kid..." The crowd surged forward, a roar of anticipation caught in five thousand throats, as Gayle leapt in an attempt to regain control of the situation, but succeeded only in heading the ball over the head of his stranded goalkeeper.

"Stu? What about him?" Neil turned to face Sutcliffe as the ball looped off Gayle's head and hung, freeze framed in the breeze, before bouncing slowly into the unguarded Sheffield goal.

Within seconds, Neil was twenty feet further down the terrace, having been hit by a tidal wave of jubilant, bouncing supporters. He struggled to remain on his feet, trampling on others who'd stumbled on the terrace steps and were now trying to regain their balance, their faces a curious mixture of terror and joy. Seeing the mass of bodies suddenly parting in front of him, Neil hauled himself upright just in time to receive a glancing blow to the forehead from a dark, gloved hand.

"Come on then you fuckers, let's have it!"

The snarling face of Andy Barton appeared inches from Neil's own. Behind him, a dozen uniformed officers wildly swung batons at the rapidly retreating fans.

"What the fuck?" Neil ducked back into the crowd as a gap appeared on the terrace between the advancing officers and the back-pedalling fans.

"Yards, get out of' way." Neil felt a hand on his shoulder and Young Sutcliffe pulled him further into the safety of the crowd.

"What the fuck's all that about? No one even did owt..."

Neil rubbed his head and found an egg-shaped bump rising above his eye, as they moved towards the side of the away terrace.

"Barton's desperate mate. Wants summat to kick off at this game so he's obviously trying to start it himself."

"He wants summat to kick off? Why?"

"Fuck knows. He's totally lost it...." Sutcliffe shook his head as Cantona unleashed a thirty yard shot which flashed across the Sheffield goal.

"Jesus, that would have sealed it. So what were you saying about our kid?"

"I heard summat." Sutcliffe reached into the pocket of his Stone Island coat and retrieved a packet of cigarettes, as a chorus of 'Ooh Ah Cantona' rang out from the Leeds end, and heavy rain began to swirl around Bramall Lane stadium.

"Heard what?"

"This is going to sound totally mad, and I wasn't sure whether to tell you..." Sutcliffe lit his cigarette and craned his neck to see Carl Shutt chasing a loose ball on the far side of the pitch.

"Well you've started now, so go on..."

Sutcliffe took a deep breath. "Word is there's some nutter harrassing Cantona. Coppers are taking it seriously. Reckon he's some sort of gangland hitman."

"Cantona? Why? And what's it got to do with our kid?"

Neil glanced back towards the pitch as a cross from the left was met by Brian Deane in the Leeds six yard box and was scrambled clear by Lukic.

"Thing is mate, coppers reckon this bloke, this hitman, they reckon he was the one who killed Stuart."

Neil paused as he digested Sutcliffe's words, and watched in silence as a long punt forward from a Sheffield defender ran out for a goal kick, before turning back to face him.

"This hitman. Any mention of a scar and a big tattoo on his neck?" Neil was shouting to make himself heard above 'We are Leeds' and a deafening crescendo of whistles, as the game drifted noisily into added time.

"Yeah, that's him. You know him then?"

"No, but I've heard of him. How do you know all this anyway?" Neil turned back towards the game as Lukic hammered a goal kick downfield and the referee looked at his watch.

"You'll find out soon enough. Everyone will."

The referee's whistle was lost in a roared outpouring of relief from the Leeds end, as the players jogged across the pitch, arms aloft and punching the air, to celebrate with the jubilant fans.

"Halfway there! Just need Liverpool to do us a favour now." Neil shouted over his shoulder. "What was that you were saying? What will everyone find out?"

He looked back towards Sutcliffe, but he was already gone. Pulling up the zip on his mustard coloured Stone Island coat, pushing his way through the ranks of ecstatic Leeds supporters, running down the steps into the concrete underbelly of the stand, and out into the terraced streets of S2.

Tears in his eyes and *'We are Leeds, we are Leeds, we are Leeds,'* ringing in his ears for the final time, knowing that after what he'd done, he wasn't anymore and never would be again.

Chapter 23

'Stay in your room', the Dutchman had said when he'd called. Apparently, Le Renard had overstepped the mark, attracted too much attention, and now leaving the UK via a legitimate route was deemed too risky. The Dutchman was arranging a small boat from the Kent coast, and in the meantime he'd been told to 'stay off the street'.

That was easy for him to say. The young man who'd followed him from the New Penny late on Thursday had smelt of rum and sweat, and Le Renard could still taste the salty perspiration on his lips when he'd woken late the following morning. The bed sheets were stained with an unidentifiable brown substance, and the vinegar scent of the cheap heroin he'd smoked before getting up had only seemed to make the room smell worse.

Opening the bathroom door had revealed the source of the stench, and the eyes of the dead youth in the bath had stared back accusingly, as Le Renard had squatted opposite the body, trying in vain to empty his bowels.

Forty eight hours later, the decomposition of the corpse had rendered the bathroom unusable, and he'd resorted to washing in the toilets of Harlequins bar. He'd resisted the temptation to leave the hotel again until Saturday evening, when the lure of the city beyond the doors of the Queens Hotel had proved too hard to resist. The promise of another night of cheap alcohol, dirty drugs and half remembered encounters with drunken, pock-faced locals slurring in their undecipherable dialect had drawn him towards the street.

Along Boar Lane, by-passing Lower Briggate and the New Penny where too many questions would be asked. Straight on towards The Calls and Kirkgate. The Duncan, The General Elliott, The Regent. No one asked questions here, as long as you could pay for a drink, no one cared. He could stay here forever, disappear. Become one of them, one of the people with their scarlet faces, their blistered lips, their market shopping bags and their piss-stained trousers. Vanish into the shadows of the darkest corners of this dirty town.

He couldn't remember returning to the room. Mud on his shoes, blood on his hands, a fog on his brain. He woke fully clothed on the bed, then held his nose as he pissed in the darkened, death stench bathroom. Then it was down to Harlequins for an early afternoon liquid breakfast.

Kieron had placed a large silver television on the bar and a group of eight middle aged men were sat facing it in a semi-circle.

"Ah here he is now!" Kieron smiled and the men turned to look Le Renard up and down as he entered the bar. He noticed a man in a purple V-necked golf jumper smirk and mutter something to the man alongside him, and Le Renard tapped the Glock in his jacket pocket and felt the reassuring bulge of the hunting knife down the back of his jeans.

"The usual is it?" Kieron already had the glass beneath the Labatts pump and the Frenchman attempted to reply but no words appeared, and he was engulfed by a hacking coughing fit which culminated in him expelling a thick paste of green mucous into an ash tray.

"I guess you'll be celebrating are you?" Kieron grimaced and nodded towards the television where two men in dark jackets were sat in a glass box in a crowded sports stadium. Between them was a slender silver trophy with ornately carved handles and a figurine on the top. The younger, dark haired presenter was listening attentively as the older man, with brushed back, fair hair was speaking, competing against a background of loud chanting.

"Celebrating what?" Le Renard reached for his drink and downed half a pint in one gulp before picking up the brandy chaser.

"Thirsty are you?" One of the semi-circle grinned until Le Renard faced him, and he fell silent and turned away.

"Celebrating the result at Sheffield! Leeds are four points clear. If Man U lose this, Leeds are champions."

"Champeones, champeones, ole ole ole!" The semi-circle raised their glasses and burst into song.

"So? I don't care about this." Le Renard finished his pint and gestured for Kieron to refill his glass.

"But your friend Eric, he made a real difference when he came on today. Did you not see the game?"

"He is not my friend." Le Renard picked up his drinks and moved away from the bar. He took up position at a table in the far corner, enjoying the gloom of the circular room, its lack of windows removing any distinction between night and day. Normally quiet, with a smattering of unimpressed hotel guests and hardcore drinkers, today Le Renard found the presence of an increasing number of drunken football supporters an irritation, as they began to loudly join in with chants crackling through the television speakers.

"Fuck all, you're gonna win fuck all!" They stood and raised their glasses and punched the air, and Le Renard

ran the cold steel of the hunting knife across his palm and struggled to contain the urge to calm himself by spilling some blood.

It was clear the match had begun, and the semi-circle had now expanded to around twenty drinkers who crowded around the television on the bar, drinks in hand, gesticulating and shouting. Le Renard decided to leave and find somewhere he was less likely to lose control and attract further attention. As he passed the bar he waved to Kieron, who responded by raising a full pint of lager.

"Come on, it's on the house!"

Le Renard backtracked and accepted the drink, nodding his thanks reluctantly. As he turned and headed back towards the corner of the room, the crowd around the TV let out a huge roar of encouragement and anticipation, before erupting into a bedlam of thrown drinks and cavorting embraces around the bar. It was clear their favoured team had scored. He glanced across towards the TV Set and saw men in red shirts celebrating, blue and white shirts slumped, dejected, defeated. He was about to turn away when a small rectangle appeared in the top left hand corner of the screen, superimposed upon the main picture.

Four men on a sofa, sitting behind a mahogany table of coffee mugs, all looking to the left, away from the camera. He first recognised the tall blond man nearest the camera from the football stadium. Then his gaze shifted right and there was Eric, wearing a blue t-shirt, slouching, looking almost disinterested, his head lower than the two men seated to his left. Le Renard was surprised to feel his heart leap again and he pushed his way through the chanting, dancing throng of supporters towards Kieron who was exchanging high fives with two men at the other side of the bar.

"Where is this?" Le Renard pointed to the screen.

"Anfield, Liverpool mate. Fuck me, we're going to win the fucker today, so we are!"

"These men are in Liverpool?" Le Renard was leaning over the bar, trying to understand what the barman was saying amidst the chaos.

"Who? The Leeds players? No, they're not in Liverpool, they're at Chapman's house."

"Where is that? How far?"

"I don't know mate, Wetherby or somewhere I guess..." Kieron was trying to serve drinks while also glancing at the TV screen. Le Renard wasn't close to the top of his list of immediate priorities until the Frenchman leant across the bar and grabbed hold of his throat.

"You tell me where that place is now, or I'll cut your fucking throat."

"Woah man, there's no need for that. I thought we were pals." Kieron managed to release Le Renard's grip and staggered back out of his reach. "Lads, where is that? Where does Chapman live?"

"Boroughbridge." The man in the purple golf jumper seemed confident.

"Write it down." Le Renard pointed at Kieron and turned back to the man.

"Is that here, in Leeds? How far?"

"No pal, up the A1. Maybe 25 miles, forty minutes at this time on a Sunday."

"How long is left in the match?" Le Renard turned back to Kieron and took the piece of paper with the name of the North Yorkshire town scrawled on it in biro.

"Over an hour to play, plus half time."

"Good, I have time. Thank you. And I'm sorry." Le Renard swilled down his drink, patted the Glock in his jacket, and dipped his room key deep into the bag of powder as he walked out of Harlequins bar.

He knew now that his actions had set Eric upon the wrong path. Today he would put that right. Today Eric would listen to his story and understand the sacrifices Le Renard had made. Recognise that without Le Renard, he may never have followed the path he had, never have become a living God. He'd listen to the story and he'd say thank you. But Le Renard would have to explain that it was too late now. Too late for them both.

There was only one path left to take now and it was better if they walked it together. The ghosts were preparing to greet them, and they laughed louder than they ever had, and clapped their blood soaked hands in anticipation.

Chapter 24

"Fucking hell Hursty, I thought you said you had a big telly!"

"It's big enough when there's just me and our lass, but it seems smaller with fifteen lads crammed into the room."

The M1 from Sheffield had never seen such a rapid evacuation, and the victorious cavalcade of cars, vans and coaches had sped north, to the sound of a fanfare of car horns and the sight of 'Champions' banners hung from every motorway footbridge. Hursty's van had arrived back in South Leeds just before the kick off at Anfield, ahead of the occupants of Jamie's car, who turned up twenty minutes into the match.

"What kept you lot? Scousers are 1-0 up." Hursty called, as an additional five somehow managed to squeeze into his small living room.

"Yeah, we've been listening. Fucking Sutcliffe disappeared. Neil wanted to wait for him." Jamie didn't look too happy.

"Eh? You wanted to wait for Sutcliffe?" Hursty looked at Neil for an explanation, but his mate just shook his head and opened a can of beer.

"Good goal was it?"

"Rush. Took it well, Scum have bottled it, you can see it in the bastards' eyes. Carpet and' ceiling are fucking soaked, our lass is going to go mental." Hursty smiled. "I bet Leslie Ash has had a word with them four, they hardly reacted at all."

"What four is that?"

"Chapman, Batty, Mcallister and Cantona are at Chapman's house in Boroughbridge. They've got ITV cameras there."

"What, now? It's live?" Neil swigged from his can as he perched on the edge of a coffee table.

"Yeah, it's all a bit weird. Mcallister's suited up and the rest are in tracksuits and stuff. They all look well embarrassed."

"And Cantona's definitely there?"

"Yeah, doesn't look like he knows what the fuck's going on." Hursty laughed as one of the lads passed him another can.

"Hursty, I need to borrow' van." Neil put down his beer and held out his hand.

"What? Yeah course, where you going? You aren't going to miss this...?" Hursty fumbled in his pocket to retrieve the van keys and tossed them across the room to Neil.

"Got somewhere I need to be, I'll catch you all later. Hopefully we'll be champions by then!"

Chapter 25

The old car park attendant had peered from his wooden shed under the arches beneath the Queen's Hotel, and squinted at the piece of paper Le Renard had thrust towards him."

"Boroughbridge? The town near York?"

"Yes, I think so. Please hurry." The tall foreigner was visually agitated, his jaw twitching and a residue of white dust coating his nostrils and speckling the beads of perspiration on his upper lip.

The old man had puffed out his cheeks, then removed his cap and scratched at his thinning hair.

"Well now you're asking. Boroughbridge. Eeeeh, well, it's off the A1. Now, the best way to get there from here, what with the one-way system..."

"Please, I have a map, I just need to know how to reach the A1." Le Renard had shifted his weight from foot to foot, leaning into the hut as the old man recoiled from his fetid chemical breath.

"Yes, well that's the problem. Probably York Road is best. Do you know how to get to the inner ring road?"

The expression on Le Renard's face had told the old man that he clearly didn't.

"Please, you show me. I will pay you." Le Renard had reached into his jacket pockets and produced a handful of twenties, but the old man shook his head.

"I don't knock off till six. I'm sorry, but I need to get home to feed my dog then too. She's blind and diabetic, I can't leave her."

Le Renard had considered increasing the monetary reward, but the clock was ticking, and he had no time to waste negotiating with the old man.

The appearance of the Glock pointed at his forehead had soon changed the car park attendant's mind, and less than ten minutes later he'd sunk to his knees and cried tears of relief, as the scarfaced Frenchman had shoved him out of the car beside a bus stop on the A64. Twenty minutes after that, the Renault was screeching around a roundabout and looping back under the A1 to arrive at a sign reading 'Welcome to Boroughbridge, Historic Town, Please Drive Carefully.'

He took the first exit, passing a sign for Green Hammerton and heading into a housing estate of brick built semi-detached houses.

"Fuck!!" Le Renard clenched his fists and hammered on the steering wheel. He'd expected Boroughbridge to be a tiny village where it would be easy to locate the footballer's house. This was clearly the outskirts of a small town. He slammed the car into third and accelerated along the long, straight road, then screeched to a halt and reversed back to the gateway of a garden centre where an elderly couple were chatting to a man with a small white dog.

Le Renard wound down the passenger side window of the Renault.

"Where is the footballer's house?"

Three expressionless faces stared back silently.

"The footballer. Leeds United. Where is his house?"

One of the men muttered something to the woman and she stooped to look into the car.

"Who are you?"

"It doesn't matter. I need to find the house. Please..."

The man said something under his breath and the dog owner nodded. All three regarded him with suspicion and remained silent.

"Fuck you! Fucking idiots." Le Renard crunched the car into first gear and accelerated down the road to another roundabout, where he followed signs to the town centre. More small houses and shitty old cars and workmen's white vans. This wasn't the sort of place a footballer would live. Those fucking idiots in Harlequins bar had clearly sent him to the wrong town. If he didn't find Eric here, he'd go back there and order a pint and a brandy, then slit all their fucking throats and watch them bleed out like pigs.

Le Renard took a right turn and sped along a narrow road with cars parked on either side, which resulted in the Renault losing both wing mirrors, as it accelerated towards a small white building ahead. A red sign caught the Frenchman's attention as he passed, and he slammed on the brakes and screeched to a halt twenty yards past the building. 'The Black Bull'. A pub. They'd be sure to know if the footballer lived nearby.

He pushed the gear stick down to locate reverse and accelerated backwards. A loud bang preceded the Renault coming to a sudden halt, before stalling then rolling slowly forward. In the rear-view mirror he could see a man in a flat cap with straggly white hair, behind the steering wheel of a blue pick-up truck. The old man was mouthing silent, angry words while shaking his head. Le Renard allowed the Renault to roll to the kerbside and got out to assess the damage. The rear bumper was hanging off and the boot had concertinaed, causing the back window to shatter. The damage appeared to be cosmetic, and he was about to get back into the driver's seat when he noticed that the offside rear wheel arch had disintegrated and the tyre was deflated.

"What the bloody hell were you doing? You shouldn't be reversing on a corner..." The old man was out of the pick-up and surveying the damage, stooping to observe a slick of oil forming on the road beneath the crumpled engine compartment of his vehicle.

"Where does the footballer live?" Le Renard reached into his jacket pocket and retrieved the packet of white powder into which he dipped the Renault key, before sucking up the scooped pile into his left nostril.

"Who? What footballer? Are you insured...Have you been drinking?" The old man watched as the scarfaced foreigner wiped the white dust from his nostrils and licked the residue from his finger before turning and striding towards the pub door.

"Where are you going? I need your details...excuse me!" The old man scurried in Le Renard's wake as he ducked through the narrow doorway to emerge in a long, empty room with an unlit hearth on the left. Directly ahead, four elderly men in woollen cardigans perched on stools, watching a small portable TV on the bar. Le Renard heard the buzz of a football stadium and glimpsed the red shirts and the blue shirts moving on the small screen.

Only the balding man behind the bar, wearing a tie and glasses, turned to observe the stranger who now stood before him, his jaw twitching and eyes staring, wide and unblinking.

"Afternoon Geoff. What brings you in at this time?" The barman craned his neck and looked beyond Le

Renard to the old man in the cap who had now followed him through the pub door.

"This bloody lunatic just reversed into me as I came round the corner, then he took off without giving me his details..."

"Do you know, we thought we heard a bang didn't we?"

The barman addressed the four drinkers who now all turned to regard the scarfaced foreigner who stared back at them, breathing heavily through white lined nostrils.

"Much damage Geoff?" One of the old men furrowed his brow and gulped the froth off his pint.

"I've not had the bonnet up yet, but it was a right bloody whack, I'll tell you..."

"Fucking shut up, all of you!" Le Renard exploded with rage, putting his hands to the sides of his head. "What is wrong with you people? Fucking imbeciles!"

The drinkers looked silently at each other, then towards the barman who began to move towards a gap in the bar on the left.

"I'm afraid I'm going to have to ask you to leave. We don't tolerate bad language in this pub at any time, let alone on a Sunday..."

"Just tell me where the footballer lives, and I will leave."

Le Renard slowly withdrew the Glock from within his jacket and levelled it at the forehead of the barman, who stopped and staggered backwards, hands held aloft. The four drinkers at the bar froze, and the pick-up truck driver ducked and shuffled backwards out of the door and onto the street.

"The footballer. Where does he live?" Le Renard felt his heart thumping and heard the quiet laughter of the ghosts. He knew the easiest way to slow his pulse, to calm himself, but killing these old men in this small town would attract attention too quickly. He hadn't had time to study the layout of the place and the local police would surely arrive before he had located the footballer's house.

"The footballer for Leeds United. I don't remember his name. He lives in this town. Tell me where, and I'll allow you to live ..."

"We're not sure who you mean." The barman spoke slowly and deliberately, looking at the drinkers across the bar. "Do any of you chaps know of a footballer living in Boroughbridge?"

"No, can't think of anyone." They scratched their heads and looked down into their pints.

"I think you're lying. I think you know." Le Renard stepped forward, the Glock now pointing at the temple of the closest drinker, who shrank away, his eyes tightly closed. From outside the pub came a mechanical stutter as the old man unsuccessfully tried to start the pickup truck.

"You give me no choice..." Just saying the words slowed the thumping in his chest, the calmness descending with the familiar anticipation of a kill.

"Lee Chapman." A small voice came from the far corner of the room.

Le Renard turned to see an old man in a brown anorak and flat cap, with a grey terrier sitting at his feet.

"The footballer you're after...It's Lee Chapman. Plays for Leeds. He's just been on the telly with that Batty lad and another one. And that French fellow. They're at his house now."

"Yes!" Le Renard strode across the room and the terrier stood up, wagging.

"He lives here, in Boroughbridge, yes?"

"No, not Boroughbridge." The old man shook his head, and his dog extended a paw towards the tall man looming over his master.

"Fuck! Shit! Those bastards. I will fucking kill them all..." Le Renard waved the Glock above his head and the men at the bar all ducked instinctively.

"Roecliffe." The old man picked up his half pint glass and took a sip.

"What?"

"He lives at Roecliffe with his wife, that actress. The blonde girl. What's her name Gerry?" The old man looked towards the bar.

"Where is this place, Roecliffe?"

"Roecliffe? It's the other side of the A1. What's her name Gerry, she was in that comedy thing with the chap with big ears..."

"Forget his fucking wife, this is important." Le Renard stooped low towards the old man who cowered at his raised voice.

"I'm sorry for shouting, I'm sorry. How far away is this Roecliffe?"

"Just over a mile would you say Gerry? Maybe a mile and a quarter?"

"Okay, thank you. So it is here...Eric is here." Le Renard knew he was close now, he could almost feel

Cantona's presence again. A different type of redemption was close, and the ghosts chuckled and clapped in anticipation.

"Which way to Roecliffe? And if you lie to me again, I'll blow your fucking face off." He turned towards the bar and the landlord pointed back down the road in the direction Le Renard had come from.

Outside the pub, the old man was still trying to start his van, and he threw his hands over his face and ducked down into the footwell as le Renard emerged through the pub door.

"Don't shoot me, please, my wife is disabled, she relies on me."

"Roecliffe. The house of the footballer Chapman. It's this way?" Le Renard pointed down the road and the old man nodded.

"It's a small place? Will I find the house easily?"

"Turn right after the pub. I'm guessing there'll be a TV van outside. It's a long walk though. Neither of these cars are going anywhere soon."

"Walk? There is no time for walking today, old man. You think I can't run?" The Frenchman tucked the pistol into the inside pocket of his jacket.

"Who are you anyway? Why are you going to his house?" The old man called after Le Renard as he set off jogging down the road, and the gangly figure paused and turned and slowly walked back towards him.

"Who am I? That's a good question... I never knew before but now I think I do. They will ask you after today... the police and the media, who was this man, what did he say to you, why did he do the terrible things he did? You understand?"

The old man removed his flat cap and scratched at his straggly white hair.

"Geoff...You're name is Geoff?"

The old man nodded, and shrank back into the cab as Le Renard approached.

"Well, Geoff, listen to me and tell them when they ask you. Tell them that I was a guardian angel who turned into a devil, and now it's time for me to return to hell."

The tall stranger with the scarred face and the fox tattoo smiled at the old man, then set off running down the road.

Chapter 26

Neil hadn't planned to go to Garforth. Going home hadn't even crossed his mind as he'd rattled up York Road in Hursty's van. It seemed almost a subconscious decision when he'd swung into the right hand lane, out past the City Lights pub, under the railway bridge and up Selby Road.

Approaching the Irwin Arms he was in two minds whether to turn round and head back down to the A64. What good would come of going home and digging up the box from the back garden for the second time in a week? Removing the old towel again and unwrapping Scouse John's gun? Why was he even going to Boroughbridge, to try and find the man who had killed his brother? Even if he showed up at Chapman's house, what good would it do?

Neil pulled the van into the car park of the Brown Cow and watched the flashes of green and blue and red from the Liverpool game reflecting off the windows in the tap room.

He drummed his fingers on the steering wheel and watched two lads in Evening Post logo Leeds shirts jog into the pub clutching bottles of lager transported from the Travs. He knew what he needed to do. Go into the pub and catch the end of the game. Watch Liverpool beat Man United to confirm Leeds as Champions. Then back into town to meet the lads. Home to Julie, laughing and bollocking him for being pissed. 'You won't be doing this when the baby comes.'

He knew what he needed to do, but still found himself turning left out of the car park, shaking his head as he turned right at the roundabout, pushing sixty on the mad-mile, past the Old George and Sunday lunch punters hurrying home to catch the end of the match, wondering if Julie would be home, but hoping she wouldn't.

She opened the door smiling.

"What are you doing here? I thought you'd be watching the match...why are you in Hursty's van? What's that lump over your eye?"

Her smile disappeared when she saw his face, as he dodged her stare and walked round the side of the house towards the back garden. Into the shed to retrieve the spade, then past the rotary dryer, to the flower bed where he'd buried Marmaduke the cat and a metal box with a gun wrapped in a towel.

"Please Neil, No. Why? What's happened?"

"I have to, I'm sorry." He couldn't look at her, as the blade of the spade broke the earth and he began to dig.

"Have to what? Please Neil, tell me what's happening, you're scaring me."

"The man who killed Stu, I think I know where he is. Where he's going to be..." The sound of metal on metal told them he'd located the box that he'd re-buried less than a week earlier.

"No...No. Please don't. Think of us, think of the baby." Julie grabbed his arm as Neil tugged the box from the soil.

"I don't know. Don't even know what I'm going to do, but I have to see him. Have to understand why..."

"No you don't! Why do you have to understand? It won't bring Stu back. He's gone Neil, you have to leave it." Tears streamed down Julie's cheeks as Neil removed the towel from the box and opened it to reveal the converted starter pistol he'd been handed at Birch Services two years earlier.

"I can't leave it Julie, I'm sorry."

"But we got a second chance. You said it yourself. No one is after us for Connolly, we got away with it...I got away with it. Don't screw it all up now Neil, please!"

"I'm sorry. I have no choice, I have to go..." Neil tucked the gun into the back of his jeans and Julie watched as he got into the van, fired the ignition into life and headed out of the cul-de-sac, without looking back.

Foot down on the A63, the flat, featureless arable land straddling the road more typical of the landscape of East Yorkshire than West. Neil had never felt at home in Garforth. Too far out. Go any further and they didn't even talk like they were from Leeds. Allerton Bywater, Normanton, Darrington and Featherstone. That far out and you might as well be from Barnsley. He'd already tried to persuade Julie to move. 'Maybe when the baby comes,' she'd said. He needed to be back in the city. In an LS postcode that began with a 1. Not Beeston or Holbeck but somewhere South or West, a nice semi inside the Ring Road, Wortley or Farnley maybe.

When the baby comes. His first child, their future. And now here he was, pulling onto the A1 with a gun hidden in his jeans, racing towards the man who'd murdered his brother. A man he'd never even seen. A hired killer who may be on a mission to murder Leeds United's star striker.

"Fuck! What am I doing?!" Neil looked at himself in the van's rear-view mirror, but kept his right foot pressed hard down on the accelerator.

He turned on the radio and twisted the dial until he detected familiar words crackling through the speakers 'Ince...Pallister...Saunders...Houghton...rocky spell for both clubs...No wins in seven games for Liverpool...one goal in their last five...but when these two sides meet..."

It was only as he pulled off the A1 and down the slip road to a roundabout, that it occurred to Neil that he'd never been to Boroughbridge in his life. Had no idea how big the place was or the location of Chapman's house. As he followed a long road surrounded by housing estates, he realised that without the assistance of locals, finding it would be a near impossible task, and the streets seemed near deserted. A pensioner pulling a shopping trolley, a young mother with a child in a pushchair, Neil slowed down alongside them, but it seemed unlikely they'd know who the Leeds striker was, let alone where he lived.

The housing alongside the road slowly gave way to a smattering of small businesses – a hairdresser, sandwich shop and Indian takeaway, then on the right, The Crown Hotel. Neil indicated and pulled over on the double-yellows opposite the large, white corner building. An old man in a wheelchair was being helped through the doorway, but beyond that, there were no signs of life from within the building.

It looked more like a hotel than a football pub, and Neil began to wonder how the locals would react to a stranger asking questions about the town's resident celebrity.

The radio commentary reported twenty minutes remaining at Anfield with Man Utd piling on the pressure. Kanchelskis won a throw-in by the corner flag, and Neil paused as Mal Donaghie launched the ball towards the penalty box. He held his breath as the frantic commentary described Mark Wright rising to head the ball clear, and Neil breathed a sigh of relief and pulled away from the kerb. Twenty minutes to the title.

"Fucking stupid." He muttered under his breath.

Why had he come here? The whole plan had been ridiculous, and he cursed himself for missing one of the greatest afternoons in Leeds United's history to chase a phantom.

As he approached a bridge, he glanced left and saw bench tables in front of a long building with mock Tudor frontage. A black sign with gold lettering above the door read 'The Three Horse Shoes.' Neil's feeling that this place looked more likely as a source of useful information was confirmed when a Ford Escort pulled into a parking space opposite the pub, and four lads piled out, one wearing a yellow Top Man Leeds away shirt.

Neil wound down the window as they jogged across the road in front of him towards the pub door.

"Have they got' game on in here lads?"

"We hope so. Just got back from Sheffield. Fucking puncture on the M1!"

"Quick question, and it might seem a weird one, but I've got to take summat to the ITV crew...where's Chapman's house? I think I've taken a wrong turn."

Three of the lads continued towards the pub but the driver stopped and pointed back down the road.

"He lives in Roecliffe mate. Back down here and look for Roecliffe Lane on the right. Follow it back under the A1. You'll see the Crown pub in the village and follow the road round right. You'll probably see the TV vans then."

"How far?" Neil felt a surge of excitement and fear. It was back on.

"Five minutes driving, it's not far. And if you get to meet him, tell him to come into town later, it's going to be a right night!" The lad pumped his chest with his right fist and ran to join his mates in the pub as Neil span the wheel and set off back down the road towards the A1.

Chapter 27

He was out of shape, he knew that. The city of Leeds seemed to have slowly eroded his mental capacity, and now Le Renard was also struggling physically. His chest felt tight, and his saliva seemed to have turned into a foamy, amphetamine paste which was causing his tongue to swell in his mouth. A searing pain flashed across his forehead and down into his eyes as he stopped running and bent to vomit on a grass verge.

A mile, the man in the pub had said, but this road seemed never ending. Long and straight with scattered farmhouses behind high hedge rows. He'd decided to hijack a car as soon as he'd passed beneath the A1 flyover, but the few that passed had been driven by old folk, who'd slowed down to peer at the wild-eyed figure waving them down, before accelerating quickly away.

Word of the incident at the pub had obviously reached the local police, but luckily the fucking fools couldn't resist a rare chance to employ their sirens, and he'd heard the two cars approaching long before they'd reached him, giving him time to duck out of sight behind the hedge.

Wiping the vomit from his mouth, he set off running again, his heart pounding and flashes of bright white light and searing pain causing him to blink with every laboured step. This endless fucking road. It was clear no car was going to stop so he decided to shoot the next driver, to bring one to a halt, but the road ahead became a confused kaleidoscope of swirling colours as he tried to focus on an approaching Range Rover. He couldn't even hold the Glock level as the vehicle approached, horn blaring, and swerving to narrowly miss him. He set off running again, the left side of his face numb and a drool of saliva and vomit coating his chin. Dazzling strobe lights in his head flashing in time with every laboured step, the sky flickering black and red.

It wasn't long before the ghosts came, as he knew they would. The fat, bearded, cartel traitor from Guadalajara. The wheelchair-bound lady magistrate from Medellin. The insider trader from Shanghai. All sitting around his mother's kitchen table, as she served them a tray of lemon tea and homemade Pastis Landais, smiling as the blood poured from her ruptured abdomen and splashed onto the ochre floor tiles. The sound of their laughter echoed in his head as he ran, but he no longer felt any hatred towards them. After all, soon he'd be joining them, and now he laughed too. Struggling for breath as he ran the endless road, but laughing through his laboured gasps, the ghosts urging him on, to finish what he'd started. The Austrian scientist, the Chechen warlord, the Icelandic fishing magnate, all drinking his mother's tea and enjoying her homemade cake, with their missing limbs, their flame scorched faces, their eviscerated torsos.

"Je rentre à la maison, maman! Je serai bientôt là." Not long now, then he'd be home, back with her again, and all this would be over.

The endless road stretched ahead of him, and Le Renard staggered on, staring with unblinking eyes at the black sky turning red. Eric was close now, he could feel the connection again and knew that soon they'd walk the path together. The only path left. He'd bitten through his own tongue and the blood dribbled down his chin, bubbling on his lips as he laughed out loud. He grasped the Glock tightly in his right hand as he ran, straddling the white line in the centre of the road.

"J'arrive Eric. Je suis le Diable et je t'aime!" A sudden searing pain from deep within his rib cage caused him to gasp for breath and clutch at his chest, and the ghosts laughed ever louder and clapped their blood-soaked hands, their cheers echoing in his head.

"Pourquoi est-ce que je t'aime? Je ne sais pas pourquoi, mais je t'aime... et je suis là maintenant."

Le Renard stopped running and stood in the centre of the road, looked up to the black sky turning red and roared like an animal through his tears.

"Sauve-moi, maman, sauve-moi!"

Chapter 28

Neil leant forward in the driver's seat and tugged the pistol from the waist band of his jeans and placed it on the passenger seat. He was still unsure what he planned to do upon encountering Stuart's killer, but it made sense to be prepared.

The radio commentary disappeared momentarily as the van passed beneath the A1, with Liverpool attacking down the right wing, with Barnes finding Houghton who picked out Molby in the penalty area. Neil turned up the volume just in time to hear Schmeichel palm the ball to safety.

"Go on Liverpool" Neil urged under his breath for the first time in his life, as the long, straight road opened up before him and he increased the pressure on the accelerator.

Pushing sixty as the road passed scattered houses behind high hedge rows, the radio crackling, reception dropping in and out.

'We're well inside the last five minutes now....'

Past a horsebox sales outlet and a campsite.

'....as Thomas makes one of those surging runs from midfield...'

Neil felt his heart thumping in his chest as the road turned into a bend. Must be close now.

'...shaking off even his own team mates.'

A section of road lined by tall poplar trees. A tall figure swaying in the road ahead.

'Thomas plays it across the face of the goal...'

The volume of the commentary increased as the figure turned to face the oncoming vehicle.

'Houghton...Off the bar...!'

The figure slowly raised his right hand, pointing it at the approaching van.

'It's there! Put in by Walters...and now the title goes to Leeds United without any doubt whatsoever.'

Neil paused momentarily, and their eyes met. Then he slowly and deliberately pushed his right foot down hard to the floor and closed his eyes.

Chapter 29

'Oh Scum, look what we've gone and done,

We've won division one,

We are the Champions.'

It was a song Neil had never heard before , but the whole city seemed to have learnt it in the couple of hours he'd spent in Boroughbridge, and it rang out from the open door of every pub as he jumped out of a taxi on Boar Lane and began trying to track down his mates.

He couldn't get through the door of Spencer's, now calling itself Q Bar, and crowds of beer-soaked revellers spilled out onto the pavement from the Prince of Wales and the Scarborough Taps.

Next, he picked his way through a hundred table-top singers in the upstairs bar at Jacomelli's. Hursty and the others weren't in, but he joined a group of lads from Bramley to throw down a couple of pints of Holsten Pils and join in some old-school classics.

"There's a red-headed Tiger known as Billy,

And he goes like a human dynamo"'

Then it was up Albion Street and down the steps to Oscars where he was soaked by flying beer during a drunken and over exuberant rendition of 'Champeones!'

It was clear that the usual town circuit had been abandoned and it was a case of going anywhere you could get a drink, and Neil eventually spotted Hursty standing on a table in the Pack Horse, arms aloft and midway through a chorus of Marching on Together.

"Yards! Fucking hell mate, we did it!" He launched himself from the bar stool and enveloped his old mate in a drunken embrace.

"Honestly Neil, did you ever think, when we were going to all those shithole grounds in the eighties, getting beat every week by fucking Grimsby and Carlisle that we'd see a day like this our lifetimes?" Hursty was slurring in his ear as someone passed Neil a bottle and ruffled his hair.

"I didn't, no. But experiencing all those horrible times makes this so much better doesn't it? I just wish Stu was here to see it."

"Fucking hell, yeah. It's like a tribute to him though maybe?" Hursty saw the tears appear in Neil's eyes and rapidly changed the subject. "Where did you go anyway? Can't believe you missed' end of ' scum game. You should have seen Ferguson's face...oh mate, it was fucking brilliant."

"Just had somewhere I needed to go. You know, to do with' baby and that..."

"Thought it must be summat like that. Young Sutcliffe never turned up though, no idea what happened to him....*Now we've won the title this is what we sing, we are the champions, we are the champions, sergeant Wilko's team!*" Hursty punched the air and finished his remaining half pint in a single gulp.

"What you drinking?" He waved his glass under Neil's nose and headed to the bar.

"I'll give you a hand." Neil pushed his way through the crowd and shouted in Hursty's ear as he jostled for position at the bar.

"I've got a bit of bad news mate. I've put a dent in' wing of' van. I'll sort it though."

"Ah, it doesn't matter, it's battered anyway. How did you do that?" Hursty shouted back while maintaining his focus on the barmaid.

"Hit a dog."

"Oh shit, did you kill it?" He turned round now to face Neil.

"Yeah. I checked. It was definitely dead."

"What did you do with it?"

"Just left it by' side of' road. Don't worry, there was no one around to get' reg plate or owt."

"I'm not bothered about that you nasty twat. I love dogs. I'd have taken it home and given it a proper burial." Hursty laughed as the barmaid spotted the fiver he was waving at her.

"I don't think Julie would have been right happy about that." Neil allowed himself a half smile. The day could have gone all too wrong, but now it felt like he'd literally dodged a bullet and gained some justice for Stu too. And Leeds were champions of England again.

The Pack Horse became Barneys, then the Guildford, then the Boulevard, then down to City Square, cans bought from the offy in the station as they watched Leeds fans dancing in the puddles and scaling the Black Prince statue, as a procession of cars flying hastily printed 'Champions' flags passed in a horn-blasting cavalcade.

Someone mentioned a Title-winning party at Yel Bar and the group were making their way up Park Row, when Rob Slater staggered up the steps from the Bank and shouted across the road.

"Fucking hell lads, have you heard?"

The blank expressions told him they obviously hadn't.

"I've just seen Tony Sutcliffe. Said his kid's in' LGI."

"What? Sheff United lads? Not heard of owt kicking off after' game." Hursty dodged a taxi and swayed across the road to meet Slater.

"No, not Sheff United, something much worse. According to his kid, Young Sutcliffe came home from' match, went straight to his room and tried to top himself."

Chapter 30

Friday 1 May 1992

Los Angeles Mayor Thomas Bradley last night signed an order for a dusk to dawn curfew for the areas most affected by rioting, after a jury acquitted four officers of the Los Angeles Police Department charged with using excessive force in the arrest of Rodney King. The incident had been videotaped and has since been widely shown in television broadcasts. By mid-morning, violence appeared widespread and unchecked as extensive looting and arson were witnessed across Los Angeles County. Rioting moved from South Central LA, north through Central Los Angeles, decimating the neighbourhoods of Koreatown, Westlake, Echo Park, and Fairfax before eventually reaching Hollywood.

"Come in Sergeant Barton close the door please." Chief Inspector Philip Holloway reclined in his seat, placed his hands behind his head, stretched, and exhaled loudly.

"It's Inspector, Sir." Andy Barton shuffled into the office, his excuses regarding the non-events of the previous Sunday well-rehearsed in his head, in anticipation of this inquisition.

"Sit down please Sergeant." Holloway's eyes flicked disapprovingly from Barton's white Nikes, up to his blue chinos before settling on his Ralph Lauren polo shirt.

Barton took a deep breath and sat down.

"I'm glad you asked to see me sir, I was hoping we'd get an opportunity to talk earlier in the week..."

Philip Holloway raised his right hand and extended the index finger.

"Be quiet please Sergeant."

Andy Barton paused and then opened his mouth to continue, until he saw Holloway begin to shake his head.

"First things first. I'm sure you've heard on the grapevine that a body was recovered close to the A1 on Sunday, which closely matched the description of the suspect in a number of unsolved murders and the stalking incidents involving the Leeds United footballer?"

"Yes, I did hear sir, and I'm pleased that our operation at Sheffield..."

Holloway made it clear that he was speaking, not listening, and continued talking while looking at a notepad on the desk in front of him.

"Well, I've just had a phone call from Mr. Gill, the coroner. Sounds like the chap had probably collapsed in the road after overdosing on a cocktail of narcotics, and was hit by an unknown vehicle which then failed to stop. We've let Interpol know, and if they want to take it any further they can. As far as I'm concerned, the matter is closed."

"Sir." Andy Barton nodded, hoping in vain that this was the only reason he'd been summoned to his boss's office.

"Now...the last time we spoke, we discussed the need for the Football Liaison team to generate some positive news headlines, did we not?" Holloway folded his arms and narrowed his eyes. Barton had been expecting this. The key thing was not to appear too well prepared. Not let Holloway know he'd rehearsed his excuses more than a dozen times. He paused again and nodded, careful not to seem too eager to begin.

"We did sir, yes. And I'm confident that I can talk you through Sunday's events and where I feel our intelligence operation failed and can be..."

"I received a phone call this morning, Sergeant Barton." Holloway's increased volume stopped Barton in his tracks.

"A phone call sir?"

"Yes Andy, a phone call. Do you know who that phone call was from?"

"Erm..." Barton's voice croaked and the sudden perspiration on his palms caused them to stick to his chinos.

"I received a phone call from a journalist..." Holloway spoke slowly and deliberately, a vein in his temple pulsing visibly and a red patch forming across his cheeks.

"A phone call from a reporter at the News of the fucking World, Sergeant!" Holloway thumped the desk causing Andy Barton to recoil in his seat.

"...And this reporter told me he was calling as a courtesy, to inform me that they'll be running a story this Sunday." Holloway stopped speaking, his mouth half open, his head quivering visibly and his breathing clearly audible.

"I don't know sir, what...what are they saying?" Barton could feel the cold perspiration forming beneath his hairline and starting to soak the back of his polo shirt.

"They're saying they have a story. An interview with a criminal informer, who was actively encouraged to break the law by a senior officer in order to implicate and entrap others. A criminal informer who was then..."

"Sir, I think I know..."

"Fucking shut up Sergeant! I don't want to hear another word." Holloway stood and shoved his chair backwards and it bounced noisily off the wall behind his desk.

"An informer who was then threatened by his handler. Threatened that his identity would be revealed to his criminal associates." Holloway was now pacing the room behind Andy Barton, who could sense his presence but daren't turn to face him.

"A criminal informer who felt so threatened by his handler, that he attempted to take his own life. Took an overdose and tried to kill himself. A boy of just twenty one years of age."

"Sir, I didn't know about that." Barton slumped in his seat, his head in his hands. "I was just trying to get him to carry out the plan, the strategy we spoke about..."

"Be very careful what you're inferring Sergeant."

Holloway gripped the back of Barton's seat and hissed into his ear. "Don't attempt to involve anyone else in this...this...fucking PR disaster that you've caused!"

"I'll speak to the lad sir, get him to see sense. I'm sure I can get him to retract..."

Holloway moved back to the other side of the desk. His tie was askew and the red patch now extended across his forehead.

"It's over Sergeant. Forget it."

"But Chief Inspector, I'm sure I can turn this around."

Holloway retrieved his chair and sat down, thumbing through a brown A4 folder on the desk.

"You were in the canine section earlier in your career were you not?"

"Erm, as a PC sir, yes. It was through matchday duty with the dogs that I got interested in football intelligence."

"Well, there's an opening for a Sergeant's position. An instructor at the dog unit in Wakefield." Holloway removed a printed sheet of A4 from the folder and pushed it across the desk.

"I don't understand sir." Barton glanced at the sheet and pushed it back. "I've no wish to revert to the canine section or a training role. I'm a frontline officer with a specialism in football intelligence..."

"The decision has been made Andy. You'll take up your new role immediately, and the PR team will attempt to diffuse this unholy fucking mess that you've created."

"But..." Barton felt his eyes prickle and the anger rising inside him.

"It's not up for debate Andy. You can leave now." Holloway pointed towards the door and closed the folder.

"But what about the football intelligence unit? I've built it up from scratch. Leeds are in Europe next year, the potential for disorder is enormous. If I may say so, this is a huge, huge mistake Chief Inspector." Barton stood and held his hands by his sides to conceal the sweat patches which had formed around his armpits.

"We're well aware of the European involvement Sergeant. The ACC has some new ideas. We believe the era of organised hooligan firms has passed. Our focus now should be on extreme right-wing infiltration of football supporters, Combat 18 and other such groups. We need a slimmed down, more cost effective FIU, headed by some new blood with more of an insight into the changing political landscape."

Andy Barton shook his head. "So you're replacing me with some young kid from Hendon with a sociology degree?"

"Quite the opposite Sergeant. The ACC visualises the new FIO as being someone with first hand experience of the growing racism problem, perhaps a black or Asian officer."

Andy Barton struggled to contain a smirk.

"A black FIO at Leeds sir? I'm afraid that's never going to work."

Philip Holloway put on his glasses and began thumbing through a sheaf of papers, no longer looking at Barton.

"Close the door on your way out Sergeant. Oh...and give the dogs a pat from me, won't you?"

Chapter 31

Sunday 3 May 1992

The Evening Post would put the figure at 150,000. Never a paper to undersell a good story, the Sun went for 300,000 people.

'Not since VE Day have the people of Leeds been so truly United', the YEP front page would proclaim, with the Capital 'U' clearly intentional. The weather had obviously helped, and a sunny Sunday morning had prompted the city's inhabitants to stream in huge numbers into the centre to watch the new champions parade their trophy at a Civic reception in the square facing Leeds Art Gallery.

An open-top bus had transported the team from Elland Road, along roads lined with flag waving supporters, as a light aircraft buzzed in the sky above the route, trailing a banner reading 'LUFC - Top of the League'.

Through City Square, up Park Row and along the Headrow, the cheering crowds scaled bus shelters and hung from lamp posts to greet Howard Wilkinson's team, before assembling en-masse beneath the art gallery balcony, a sea of flags and scarves waved by supporters celebrating the end of eighteen years of pain.

The players appeared bewildered by the spectacle and the emotion of the day, recognising that for most of them, this would be the pinnacle of their careers.

The journeymen pro's- Sterland, Chapman, Whyte, Shutt. The youngsters -Batty, Speed, Wallace. The captain, Strachan, given a new lease of life, a chance to restart his career. The mastermind of the club's resurrection, Wilkinson, summing up the mood.

'The culmination of a dream. This is the greatest day of our lives.'

On the crowded balcony, behind the team in their matching tracksuits and club shop 'Champions' T-Shirts, behind the Lord Mayor and the civil dignitaries, stood Cantona.

He watched from the shade as his team mates were introduced to the fans one by one, by an excitable radio presenter, each taking their turn at the front of the balcony, triumphantly lifting the trophy and saying a few words to the assembled masses if they felt brave enough.

Cantona smiled as he observed them enjoying the moment. Their moment, the pinnacle of their careers, the greatest day of their lives.

Ooh-ahh Cantona, Oo-ahh Cantona!

Ooh-ahh Cantona, Oo-ahh Cantona!

Quiet at first, so he could pretend not to hear. Standing at the back, out of the glare of the lunchtime sun, sipping from a bottle of water.

Ooh-ahh Cantona, Oo-ahh Cantona!

Louder now, his team mates turning towards him and smiling. Hodge waving, Chapman laughing, shouting over in his primary school French. Batts and Speed calling him forward. The boss turning and smiling now, beckoning him to the front. He stepped forward and someone draped a Leeds scarf around his neck. The radio presenter turned and handed him a microphone.

"The people want to hear you. Just say a few words."

He approached the concrete parapet and stared out across the vast expanse of Victoria Gardens at the people of Leeds, who raised their hands and roared their approval.

Ooh-ahh Cantona, Oo-ahh Cantona!

"Just say thank you, that you're very happy."

The radio presenter shouted in his ear, but he wasn't listening. His hands gripped the microphone and he looked out at a sea of yellow, blue and white. The crowds chanting his name, the eyes of a whole city upon him, waiting to hear him speak.

"Thank you... that's all you have to say." The presenter urging louder now in his ear, but still he didn't hear. Empty platitudes were worthless, the words had to mean something and they appeared in his mind suddenly, with an absolute clarity, and he knew straight away that they were perfect.

"Pourquoi est-ce que je t'aime?"

"Why I love you?" Eric leaned over the balcony, the microphone in his hand, and as his voice filled the square, the crowd roared their approval, his team mates laughed and the presenter slapped him on the back.

Ooh-ahh Cantona, Oo-ahh Cantona!

He looked out at the sea of waving flags and swirling scarves, the people of Leeds enjoying their moment in the sunlight again after years in the darkness.

"Je ne sais pas pourquoi, mais je t'aime."

"I don't know why, but I love you." The microphone crackled and his words echoed around the square. The people cheered and Eric smiled and wondered where the words had come from, but that didn't matter as long as they were from the heart.

He removed the Leeds scarf, and handed the microphone back to the radio presenter, nodded to his grinning team mates, then headed once more to the back of the crowd on the balcony.

Standing in the shade again, out of the glare of the sun, he watched as his team mates basked in the glory of their achievement, enjoying their moment, the pinnacle of their careers, the greatest day of their lives. Leeds United, England's last league champions.

Bournemouth 90

Billy Morris

It's April 1990 and the world is changing. Margaret Thatcher clings to power in the face of poll tax protests, prison riots and sectarian violence in Northern Ireland. The Berlin wall has fallen, South Africa's Apartheid government is crumbling and in the Middle East Saddam Hussein is flexing his muscles, while Iran is still trying to behead Salman Rushdie.

In Leeds, United are closing in on a long-awaited return to the first division. Neil Yardsley is heading home after three years away and hoping to go straight.

That's the plan, but Neil finds himself being drawn back into a world of football violence, and finds a brother up to his neck in the drug culture of the rave scene. Dark family secrets bubble to the surface as Neil tries to help his brother dodge a gangland death sentence, while struggling to keep his own head above water in a city that no longer feels like home.

The pressure is building with all roads leading to the south coast, and a final reckoning on a red-hot Bank Holiday weekend in Bournemouth that no one will ever forget.

Available in Paperback and ebook in all Amazon stores.

Printed in Great Britain
by Amazon

27167434R00099